THE

SIN-SICK SOUL

D.R. LEWIS

a novella

©2020 D. R. Lewis. All rights reserved.
Printed in the Unites States of America

ISBN: 978-0-578-75773-5
Library of Congress Catalog Number: 2020919337

♥ Hood Love Press
info@hoodlovepress.com

Dedication

Me: "Girl, your life is batshit crazy. I'd write a book, but no one would believe it."

My sister: "Go ahead. I'll sue, we'll go on Oprah, stage an epic fight, and make a shitload of money. Momma will be so proud.

♥

For Delores, who sparkled too brightly for this dark world.

Preface

SOMETIMES WRITING SUCKS. And searching your soul to recast some of your most painful memories into coherent sentences? That double-sucks.

To the initiated, this statement is a big ole "duh." But where I'm from, most know little about the emotional bloodletting required to craft heartfelt prose and couldn't care less about the twisted mental gymnastics that drive so many seemingly happy, well-adjusted people to orchestrate their own deaths. In the gritty inner city, death by murder is heartbreaking, but understandable. But taking your own life? No. Self-proclaimed hood rats like my baby sister Delores live on the edge, but they don't jump. Or do they? Recent research suggests otherwise.

According to the Centers for Disease Control (CDC), suicide is the tenth leading cause of death for all ages and the second most common cause of death behind unintentional injury for people ages 25-34. More than 40,000 Americans kill themselves each year. That's more than a hundred each day or approximately one suicide every 10 minutes. Nearly 35 percent of suicide decedents test positive for alcohol, 25 percent for antidepressants (they often place crack cocaine in this category), and 20 percent for opiates, including heroin and prescription painkillers. On average, suicide costs our society an estimated $51 billion annually in medical expenses and lost work production.[1]

Furthermore, a 2020 study published in *JAMA Pediatrics* suggests that young people in high-poverty communities are even more likely to die by suicide. The analysis of nearly 21,000 deaths over a decade shows that in U.S. counties with poverty rates of at least 20 percent, people in the age range of 5 to 19 years old were 37 percent more likely to die by suicide than people in counties where less than five percent of residents lived in poverty. After controlling for factors like demographics and urban-rural status, researchers found youth suicide rates rose in a stepwise manner across five levels of county poverty concentration—as poverty rates rose, so did youth suicide rates. Given what we know about suicide trends within families, ignoring these trends could mean generational devastation for already vulnerable communities.[2]

This chasm between data and denial is why I was committed to finding a more impactful way to bring this story to light. Generic facts and figures don't resonate with these families, especially when the (most likely) intentional death occurs *not* by the victim's own hand. My hope? Maybe raw, unapologetic, and sometimes humorous storytelling will touch a nerve.

Now, a word about my chosen genre: I began keeping a journal about what we playfully titled my sister's "thug life" more than 25 years ago at the height of the U.S. crack cocaine epidemic. By 1996, the year Delores died, I had amassed such an extensive collection of jaw-dropping anecdotes that completing her memoir seemed a no-brainer. Delores and I often joked that "our book" would shock the world to both our benefits (insert sarcastic giggles here). I would shamelessly divulge her innermost secrets, she would feign outrage and sue me, and our entire family would end up yelling at the top of our lungs on what would be the season's highest-rated episode of *The Oprah Winfrey Show.*

Then Delores died, and something changed. I'm not sure why exactly, be it grief, writer's block, or good old-fashioned procrastination, but for the next 15+ years, I couldn't bring myself to touch my journals, let alone begin the arduous task of formulating the comprehensive, fact-based manuscript my sister and I had envisioned. In fact, the mere thought of staying inside my head long enough to stitch together 100,000 words chronicling one of the most painful experiences of my life made me nauseous.

Then, a few years ago, while attending my cousin's Narcotics Anonymous "clean" birthday celebration, I had an epiphany. As I scanned the crowd, conjuring stories about the plethora of life lessons that undoubtedly had delivered us all to that specific place and time, it occurred to me: why not re-imagine Delores's escapades as a novella, a compact work of fiction, consumable in one or two sittings—an intense read requiring little more time commitment than a feature film? Not only did this ease the pressure to achieve some arbitrary word count standard, but the decision also allowed me to escape reality and play fast and loose with the facts. In a word, I could detach. Overnight the dreaded project became therapy. Now only the story set the rules.

To parents, children, siblings, and friends living with someone battling addiction, I pray you strength. To my own family, and to others who have lost a loved one to any manner of self-destructive behavior, I pray you peace.

And one more thing: when you speak of that quirky, smart, funny, but hopelessly addicted spark in your life, as you remember the good times, don't be afraid to laugh out loud.

That's exactly what Delores would do.

♥

THE

SIN-SICK SOUL

Crack, chaos and a mother's
misguided search for spiritual healing

There is a balm in Gilead,
To make the wounded whole;
There's power enough in heaven,
To heal a sin-sick soul.

— Negro Spiritual, 1800s

ONE

Cursed

To the good Christian, the idea of suicide by murder is nonsensical. I mean, really, how could someone who claims to love the Lord justify taking any action to end her own life? Well, maybe if you'd met Dana back then, before everything went to shit. Then, you might understand.

♥

"DON'T SAY I DIDN'T WARN YOU. That dress is jinxed."

The Lawton girls had commandeered the dining room, striking glamorous poses in the big wall mirror, modeling outrageous hairstyles. Lenita was older by nine years, but when it came to men, without question, Dana Renee was more experienced.

"I don't believe in no stupid jinx," Dana shot back. "Just because you and Tina picked the wrong men, it doesn't mean me and Terran won't work. Your wedding dress is cute, *and* it's free. I'm wearing it."

The hand-me-down gown in question had already spawned two divorces: one for Lenita from Marcus Henry, a smart, handsome, and neurotic accountant, and one for their cousin Martina from "Jason the Great," a part-time insurance salesman and full-time liar who had left home for a client meeting two weeks after the honeymoon, never to be heard from again.

It would be tough to remember a happier time in Dana's life than those weeks before her wedding. It was 1992 in Kansas City, the city of fountains—and of contradictions. On one side of the metro were the elites: Mercedes-Benz-driving, Saks Fifth Avenue-shopping bluebloods from the hundred-year-old Ward Parkway mansions and impeccably manicured lawns in the west. On the other, east of Troost Avenue, the city's long-accepted racial dividing line was where working-class blacks like the Lawtons, the middle-poor, were "encouraged" to live. These streets were lined with more modest, pastel-colored shirtwaist houses: three stories, part wood siding and part stucco; half as old, twice as shabby. Every home had a large front porch, usually brick, and unlike the well-to-do strangers on the other side of town, in these neighborhoods, everyone knew everyone. Baptist ministers lived in contrived harmony next door to drug dealers, and the nighttime cracks of gunfire were still infrequent enough to elicit a call to the authorities.

That year—the winter of Dana and Terran—the city was experiencing some of the most brutal weather on record. For weeks, headlines warning of record-high snowfall and low wind chills, deadly auto accidents, and school closings dominated the news, but for Dana, life was all sunshine and roses. She was about to marry her man, Terran Jackson, the father of her only child, after almost ten years of "just messin" around. The two had barely been teenagers when they'd met at a middle school basketball game. For Terran, it was love at first sight; for Dana, not so much.

"He looked like a dork," she'd laugh. "Cute, but too skinny."

By now, at 26 and 28 years of age, respectively, Dana and Terran shared a partnership rarely seen in their circles. Always cracking jokes and finishing each other's sentences, the two were more than lovers; they were friends. If any relationship had the makings of a successful marriage, this was it.

In his final year of high school, a late growth spurt had catapulted young Terran from average height to well over six feet tall. Still boyishly handsome today, his chocolate-brown skin and hazel eyes were almost as attractive to the daycare moms as his quick wit and amiable smile. And it didn't hurt that he was the ultimate doting father to Terran Charles Jackson, Jr.—whom everyone called TJ—a precocious two-year-old who loved to blow spit bubbles.

In both world view and temperament, Dana was her popular boyfriend's doppelganger. For her, no topic was too serious to become the butt of a joke. She was also attractive, but in a quirky, strong-featured way. Dana was taller than the other five girls in the Lawton family, with thick, sandy hair that never seemed to cooperate. And her juicy lips, typical "black girl" butt, and big brown eyes that sparkled when she smiled made her tough to ignore. When, in her first year of community college, she discovered she was pregnant, the response was classic Dana: "Terran had better be ready to clean poop, or we're leaving this kid at the hospital."

FOR DANA AND TERRAN, if you weren't laughing, you weren't living.

One night, the sisters had been chatting on the phone for almost an hour, talking about nothing. Lenita had heard muffled voices a few times during the conversation. TJ must be fussing to get his momma's attention, she'd thought.

Out of the blue, Dana started fake-coughing, trying to stifle a giggle. "Hold on a minute, Nita. Terran's cummin'."

Lenita screamed and dropped the phone.

"Oh my God. You idiots were having sex the whole time?" Lenita said as she hung up the phone, but not before hearing Dana and Terran laugh so loud they probably woke the baby. Classic Dana.

Despite Lenita's warning, on the first Saturday in February of that winter to end all winters, her little sister wore the dress, spoke the vows, and gleefully changed her name. After a brief weekend honeymoon in the not-so-glamorous Ozark Mountains, Dana and Terran immediately set up house. As luck would have it, Terran's uncle had just been evicted from an affordable two-bedroom fixer-upper less than 20 minutes from Terran's job. The place was petite, with nicotine-stained walls and the musty smell of wet carpet, but unlike most in the neighborhood, it had a solidly constructed front porch and a chain-link-fenced backyard.

This, I can work with, Dana decided during her first visit, and then went about working her thrift-store magic. Two months and several enormous bottles of Pine-Sol later, the "stinky place," as it had come to be known by her family, became the Jackson home.

"We're in the hood but not of the hood," Dana would proudly proclaim.

Glass half full.

TWO

Stepford Wife

FOR THREE GLORIOUS YEARS, Dana lived what her family dubbed a white-picket-fence life. But that wasn't the original plan. In the fall the year of her second pregnancy, Dana was midway through a highly competitive nursing program, working towards a career in pediatrics. Although staying on the path positioned her to out-earn her husband three-fold, as soon as the baby was born, Dana slipped into the role of stay-at-home mom with ease. Truth be told, she dreaded the prospect of leaving her newborn in the hands of strangers. And unlike most of her sisters, Dana enjoyed cooking, decorating, and pretty much all things domestic. It didn't hurt that this lifestyle was exactly what Terran wanted. Throughout his childhood, he had watched his own father drift in and out of the family's lives at will, and he was determined to break the cycle.

"Daddy has to go to work," he would explain to his fidgety toddler at bedtime. "Mommies take care of home. Daddies take care of everything else." For Dana, whose father died when she was in elementary school, leaving her mother as sole breadwinner, this point of view took some getting used to.

"Old-fashioned, macho bullshit," she'd assert. "But hey, whatever floats his boat."

Egos aside, living on a high school graduate's income was tight. Yet, what some viewed as scarcity, Dana, an eternal optimist, celebrated as simplicity. Her mother and namesake, the senior Dana whom friends called Momma D, had raised 10 children on less than what Terran brought home. As Dana recalled, their childhoods had been just fine.

"Trust your husband and have faith. God will provide," Momma D had preached to all her daughters over the years. Dana could recite the relevant Bible verse at will: "I am the bread of life; whoever comes to me shall not hunger, and whoever believes in me shall never thirst." (John 6:35 ESV).

Understandably, Dana had idealized her childhood memories. As the youngest sibling, she was the favorite, especially after her father, Momma D's second husband, died of a massive stroke just three weeks shy of his 50th birthday. To feed her kids and keep the bank from foreclosing on her house, a week after the funeral,

Momma D began working two full-time jobs, forcing the older children to take on more responsibility at home.

Each night, when Momma dropped in just long enough to change clothes between shifts, the inquiry was the same: "Where's the baby? Who's watching Dana Renee? Did y'all feed that child yet?"

"She's sleeping." "We all watchin' her." "She ate good today." These were the only right answers.

As the kids got older and little Dana became more aware of her power, tensions flared. But no matter what havoc she created, woe to the brother or sister who made baby Dana cry.

"Stop pickin' on that chile, or I'll pick on you," Momma would warn.

While this pampered position in the family likely had something to do with adult Dana's insatiable need for attention, material possessions meant nothing to her. When her older sisters shunned hand-me-downs as yesterday's played-out fashions, Dana embraced every piece as something unique and retro.

Dana's overall outlook on life was equally mellow. Since she was smart, school success came relatively easy. But even when slumping grades in tough anatomy classes threatened her scholarship, she wasn't fazed. "I'll talk to the professor. We'll figure it out," she reasoned. And she always did.

Good food, a warm bed, and people who loved her: from infancy to adulthood, that's what Dana valued.

To Terran's delight—he wasn't especially materialistic either—this "don't worry, be happy" attitude had permeated their marriage—that is until the untimely arrival of their second child. The phone call from Dana's hospital bed was an experience Lenita would never forget.

"Lenita Marie, do you know where I am? Do you KNOW where I am? This is all your fault!" Dana ranted.

Holding the receiver away from her ringing ears, it took Lenita about 10 seconds to figure out why Dana was so up in arms. Her second baby was about to enter the world much earlier than Dana, Terran, the doctors—everyone except Lenita—had forecast.

"Well, it's not all my fault," Lenita teased.

Months earlier, after an uneventful prenatal visit, Dana and Lenita had been enjoying an unseasonably warm late-winter afternoon on her brightly painted front porch, looking like two beached whales. Lenita was in her ninth month, expected to pop any day. Dana was in month seven, or so the doctors had estimated.

"Since we didn't really plan this one," Dana explained, "we aren't sure of the due date. They didn't tell us the sex; we don't want to know, but his or her size suggests mid-May, maybe sooner. TJ was a chunk. Maybe this one will be big, too."

"Whatever," Lenita had said. "This baby is a boy, and he will be born April 29, one year to the day after his big brother."

And that's exactly what happened. Dana's water had broken an hour before the call as she stood in line at the grocery store.

Frustrated but not at all afraid (that's Dana), she finished her shopping, swung by the house to drop off the groceries and check in with the babysitter, and then drove herself to the hospital. By the time she reached her sister, she was already dilated to eight. Tyler John Jackson was born an hour later. At six pounds, eight ounces—a third smaller than his older brother—this little one entered the world screaming at the top of his lungs, a preview of a life spent demanding to be heard.

Before you conclude Lenita must be psychic or something, consider the family history. Shared birthday parties were a thing in the Lawton household. Momma D had borne only one set of twins, but every one of her 10 children shared their birthday month with at least one brother or sister. The last three, Dana, Roger, and Malia, had been born on the same day—May 23—one year apart. Since Dana was the first of these Irish triplets to give birth, in her sister's view, she was the one destined to carry on the tradition.

The moment the pimply-faced nurse in the emergency room placed the fussy newborn on his mother's ample breasts, Dana became obsessed. The baby was fine now, but unlike TJ, Tyler's had been a difficult birth, requiring forceps, extra anesthesia, and an incubator on standby. Almost everything about the experience had filled Dana with anxiety.

"His head looks funny, and it sounds like he's in pain. Why is he crying like that?" she asked the pediatrician on call that night.

"And his weight. TJ was so much bigger. That's not good, is it?" she fretted to her husband.

Frustrated no one seemed to be taking her questions seriously, Dana set out to find her own answers. While she had always excelled in science and math, she had never been an avid reader. If it wasn't for her gift of gab, she'd have never passed high school English. That changed after Tyler. Soon Dana had stocked her car, living room table, and bathroom with pamphlets, books, magazines, and any other "raising perfect children" resources she could get her hands on.

As her parenting knowledge and the Jackson babies grew into toddlers, Dana flipped the script; once again, she was the easygoing mom coaching her obsessive-compulsive sisters to chill out. Still, whenever the Lawton clan got together, chaos inevitably ensued.

Picture three semi-adult mothers—Lenita, Dana, and middle sister Malia, the super-aunt and organizer with no kids of her own—four rugrats under age six—TJ, Tyler, and their cousins Alex (Lenita's only child) and Ashley (daughter of middle sister Rayna, the consummate cynic)—and 14-year-old Damon, son of eldest sister, Casandra. The outings were hectic, cost more than any of them could afford, and mandatory.

"Don't worry 'bout givin' kids a lot of things; just spend time with 'em. *That's* what they'll remember," Momma D always said.

To her dutiful daughters, that meant ice-skating at the swanky downtown rink, roller coasters and cotton candy at the local amusement park, and weekend road trips to the lake just to feed the ducks. While every skinned knee or tummy ache sent Malia and Lenita into a tizzy, Dana was in hog heaven, clowning around and causing more trouble than the babies.

"What are we gonna do if it rains?" Lenita and Malia would complain. "Oh, crap! Alex spilled orange sherbet all over his new shirt! Wait! What's taking Damon so long in the restroom? And Ashley pouting again—that girl works my nerves."

The more the older sisters bitched, the more Dana teased.

"Here's an idea: let the boys finish their ice cream on the porch, and then they can play in the rain. Alex's shirt will be clean in no time. And Ashley's whining again. So what? Girls do that."

Since dads weren't invited on these excursions, the husbands had to create their opportunities to bond with their kids. For most of the dads, it was hit or miss, but not Terran. Though his work schedule was unpredictable, if he was at home, the message was clear: "Let the games begin!"

In person or on the phone, the chaos was palpable, especially in the morning: doors slamming, shoes thundering on hardwood, and too-loud growls and squeals as all the Jackson boys—Terran, TJ, and Tyler—did everything in their power to disrupt the start of the day.

"What the hell is going on over there?!" confused family members would yell into the phone.

Sometimes, to save face, Dana would at least try to feign anger.

"Really, Terran, what are you teaching them boys?!"

Silence for a few seconds, then howling laughter.

Wild, crazy, out of control—that was Dana's life, and she wouldn't have it any other way.

THREE

Warning Signs

"NITA, HAS TERRAN SEEMED WEIRD LATELY?"

Dana was on the floor with Tyler, tickling his toes and watching him giggle.

"Terran's always weird," Lenita answered. "I thought that was what made your marriage work: crazy together."

Dana laughed a little too hard for the weak joke. She wasn't worried, really. It wasn't like she and Terran weren't still into each other. Just that morning, TJ had busted them having a quickie on the kitchen table, the smell of burnt bacon filling the air.

"What up, dude! Momma and Daddy just wrestling," Terran explained, causing Dana to laugh so hard she spurted coffee through her nose.

Maybe he'd lost his temper a few times lately for what felt like trivial things. And so what if he disappeared in the middle of the day when he was supposed to be at work? Isn't it normal for a man to need his space? And, Dana thought, she could come up with a dozen explanations for the recent rash of phone hang-ups.

"Probably the ex-whoever of some brother who had this phone number before us," Dana concluded.

Dana wasn't yet ready to tell Lenita, but there was one recent development she couldn't explain away so easily. Over the past few weeks, her husband's pocket money had begun to disappear.

"Can you spot me a few dollars," he'd ask casually. "We're almost out of milk (or bread or cheese or whatever), and I don't have any cash on me right now."

He'd return hours later with no groceries and no cash.

"Girl, stop trippin'," he'd snap when she sought an explanation. "I had to take care of something. I'll get to the store before breakfast tomorrow."

When the disappearances escalated to home electronics, Terran's excuses and his overall demeanor became downright bizarre.

"I took the TV and VCR to Mike's," he barked, annoyed. "He's a bachelor, so the guys from work prefer to play cards and watch old karate movies at his house. What's the big deal? We have the same setup in our bedroom, and TJ and Tyler can watch cartoons in their room. They like that better anyway."

Soon any conversation about money drew the same over-the-top response: Dana would ask what used to be an innocent question. Terran would blow up and then clam up. Frustrated,

Dana made the uncomfortable decision to do something she swore she'd never do: spy on her husband—an act she'd always associated with insecure women.

Desperate times, desperate measures, she reasoned

Fortunately, or so Dana thought, stalking Terran should be easy. Because his shift on the line at the Chase meatpacking plant started early, 6:00 a.m., Terran was typically out of the house before the babies were even awake. The night before, all she needed to do was come to bed late and feign exhaustion so her husband wouldn't get close enough to realize she was fully dressed. She'd wait for him to drive away, and then she'd spring into action.

On that warm July morning, Terran seemed inexplicably anxious, especially given that all week, Dana had taken extreme care not to ask any of *those* questions. She lay in bed, perfectly still, waiting for the customary goodbye pat on the butt and eerie squeak of the closing screen door. When the coast was clear, she jumped out of bed.

"Wake up, baby," she coaxed TJ. "Momma's got to go out for a while."

Without turning on any lights in the house, she scooped up the diaper and TJ's still-sleeping baby brother and led her toddler out the back door, across the cracked stone walkway, and into the welcoming arms of her next-door neighbor.

"Thanks for this, girl. They'll probably sleep another hour or two," she told Nae as her friend helped arrange the boys' favorite blankets on her ratty brown sofa.

"No problem, honey," Nae whispered. "I love looking after these little monsters."

"I should be back by lunchtime, if not sooner," Dana promised, planting wet kisses on chubby cheeks.

By now, it was well past 5:30 a.m., and the city buses had started their runs. Dana looked both ways before heading towards the well-lit bus stop at the intersection of 27th and Benton Boulevard. Although she felt safe inside her house, she harbored no delusions about the ever-present danger on the streets around her. In the war on drugs, midtown Kansas City was ground zero. Dana had attended elementary school with half the crackheads living within a ten-mile radius, so she had seen first-hand how addiction could drive people to do awful things, even to people they liked. Or, as she was about to find out, to people they loved.

Dana's plan was simple: Take the 5:50 to 45th and Cleveland Avenue—Malia's apartment. She'd already convinced her sister to let her keep the car for the day. If it all worked out, she'd have just enough time to get to Nina's—a local soul food restaurant where the guys on A Shift, Terran's crew, met each morning for coffee and donuts. To find out what (or who) her husband was doing, staking out his favorite hangout was as good a place to start as any. That was the plan, at least, but as Dana would soon discover, plans change. Shit happens.

FOUR

Blindsided

A S DARKNESS GAVE WAY TO DAYLIGHT, Dana found herself power-walking on the wrong side of the street, against traffic. *Get the lead out, girl.*

If she missed the early bus, she'd never make it to Malia's in time to drop her off at work and get to the restaurant before Terran's break time was over.

Finally, just across the street from her stop, Dana unzipped her too warm windbreaker and prepared to cross. Before she could step off the curb, a sound, something between a scream and a squeal, captured her attention. It was a girl, familiar, obviously impaired, and much too animated for that time of the morning.

Dana was intrigued but hesitant. The commotion was coming from the cul-de-sac—that black hole at the mouth of her neighborhood where three crack houses shared a circular drive. Drugs Central, the church folk called it. Dana took a few steps toward the noise, pausing behind a bullet-riddled stop sign.

Shame, she thought. *There, but for the grace of God, go I.*

The sound persisted, and though she had no time for diversions, Dana's curiosity got the better of her—she *had* to investigate. So many of her once-happy, God-fearing loved ones were now "on that end"—addicted, suffering, and lost. What if this was someone she cared about, and what if that someone was in trouble?

As she stepped into the open, still at least a block away from the source of all the hoopla, Dana was confused. *Is that a dark green Honda?*

"Naw, it can't be," she said aloud to no one in particular.

By now, the 5:50 bus had come and gone, and she had reached the end of the driveway of the first house in the circle. Daylight illuminated the streets, but she couldn't see inside; green trash bags covered the windows. She paused, paralyzed, not by the eerie darkness of the structure or the half-naked hostess on the porch, but by what she'd spied inside the Honda. There, dangling from the rearview mirror, was a blue and yellow race car—Tyler's first toy, a gift from her husband when they'd discovered they were pregnant the second time.

"A house full of boy toys equals a house full of boys," Terran had predicted.

"Yeah, right," Dana had replied sarcastically. "Is that another one of your old voodoo cousin's whack mojo spells?"

Then Tyler came into the world, another boy.

"See? It works," Terran had boasted.

Her mind racing, Dana made her way around the driver's side of the car to the porch, where Giggly Girl was holding court, not at all in distress. Dana focused first on the imposing figure seated on the top step. A mountain of a man, well over six feet tall, 300+ pounds, in dark sunglasses and steel-toed boots, was casually sipping on a 40-ounce, balancing a shiny silver pistol between his knees. His partner's appearance was the exact opposite: pale, blond, emaciated, in a tailored navy-blue jacket, and dirty khakis. While you'd most likely cross the street if Mountain Man was in your path, if not for his singed fingernails, pockmarked complexion, and bloodshot eyes, Junkie #2 looked like someone you'd hire to do your taxes.

Neither lookout paid Dana any attention. She ascended the stairs in a daze, but not until she reached the heavy steel door did her eyes and mind make the connection: Giggly Girl was someone she knew well—Cousin Tina.

From the moment she hit puberty, Martina Cole was the envy of every undeveloped pre-teen female in the neighborhood. Momma Dana and Marilyn, Dana and Tina's mothers, had met at community college the summer they both turned 22. Dana's mother was studying social work, and Marilyn worked in the cafeteria. A chance meeting at the bus stop, where they swapped stories about food stamps, bus passes, and unsafe childcare, soon blossomed into the kind of unlikely sister-friend relationship only hood dwellers understand. Over the years, the two young mothers shared everything; they even had children by the same man. Instead of the vicious feud one might expect such a love triangle to provoke, with each new half-sibling, their bond grew stronger. To make things simple, all the kids, Ms. Mae's six and Ms. Dana's 10, addressed each other as "cousin." This chosen family shared more sleepovers, picnics, and Thanksgiving and Christmas dinners than anyone could count, right up until Marilyn's untimely death from ovarian cancer the summer she would have turned 40.

As adults, all the Lawton/Cole women eventually learned to appreciate their own unique gifts. But as teenagers, there wasn't one who hadn't, at some point, coveted the ample physical attributes with which God had blessed Tina, or so everyone believed.

FIVE

Father Figure

So, yeah. Pretty girl, ghetto streets. It'd be a shocker if evil didn't find her.
Still, it's tough to stomach who was leading the hunt.

♥

AT THE TENDER AGE OF 14, Tina Cole would be best described as a precocious child trapped in the body of a grown-ass woman: 36DD breasts, a tiny waist, and firm, round, child-bearing hips that compelled every full-blooded male past puberty to snap to attention. And her dark-set eyes, chocolate-brown skin, and lazy (some said *sexy*) way she drawled her words projected maturity beyond her years. Men wanted Tina. But Tina was also sweet in an over-the-top, syrupy way; in spite of themselves, most women and girls liked her. Of her many fans, no one was more adoring than Jessie Cole Sr., her garish, loud, and, until two years earlier, estranged father.

While her older brother, Jessie Jr. (JJ), never seemed to run out of tall tales about childhood antics involving his father, at that time in her life, Tina had only one early memory of Jessie Sr.: the day her parents split. It was a Sunday morning, and five-year-old Martina was parked in front of the living room window, waiting for the church bus to take her and her mother to Sunday school. To Ms. Mae's annoyance, Big Jessie had stumbled into the house only about an hour earlier, sweaty, drunk, and agitated. Tina could hear her parents fighting through the bathroom door.

"Momma, ain't it time to go yet?" Tina yelled as she skipped through the dining room toward the back of the house. Before Ms. Mae could answer outside, all hell broke loose. On Friday, Jessie had made a promise to an irate bookie: pay up or, well, *pay*. Now three men were outside the family home, riddling his precious powder-blue Lincoln Continental with bullets. Though the gunmen never took aim at the house (in those days, families were off-limits), the chaos that ensued—her parents' screams, her brother tackling her to the floor—left Tina deeply shaken. For Ms. Mae, this was the last straw.

Later that night, Big Jessie packed everything he could cram into his bullet-ridden ride and moved to Topeka, Kansas, with 12-year-old JJ in tow. Years later, Tina discovered the move had included someone else: Marva Collins, a big-butt white woman with whom her father had been having an affair for more than four years.

Over the next nine years, Jessie Sr. had parlayed his marginal street smarts, by Kansas City standards, into a kingpin position at the top of a lucrative criminal enterprise built around gambling, drugs, and for-sale women. He was now a big fish in a small pond, with no nagging wife to challenge him. Not surprisingly, there was no space in his life for a toddler, especially a girl. But for young JJ, a cocky pre-teen, life couldn't have been better.

While Ms. Mae rarely spoke of her husband's illicit activities, she was determined to keep tabs on her son, insisting on frequent calls and regular weekend and summer visits. But since the night he left, Big Jessie and Tina's relationship had devolved into no more than a holiday chat or occasional cash gift passed on from her mother. About Big Jessie's sordid lifestyle, Tina had no clue. One warm Saturday, the morning of her 16th birthday, this would abruptly change, and not for the better.

It was 7:00 a.m., too early for Tina and cousin Lenita to be awake, dressed, and *bouncing off the walls,* as Ms. Mae described them. After months of weekend babysitting and selling their state-funded lunches for cash, the girls had finally scraped together enough money for what would be the party to end all parties. They had already reserved the gigantic table at the old Skateland roller rink in midtown. For weeks, Tina had been handing out Lenita's colorful, hand-drawn flyers. Since the party was happening on Saturday, everyone who mattered would be there anyway, but Tina wasn't taking any chances. Lenita had also made decorations, which was one reason she'd slept over the night before. Ms. Mae and Ms. Dana would provide the food: fried chicken, greens, macaroni and cheese, homemade rolls, and sweet tea—no skimpy finger food for *this* bash. There was even a huge cake topped with what was supposed to be a blue eagle, Tina's school mascot, courtesy of Ms. Ophelia, the blind-in-one-eye, can't-see-out-the-other ex-pastry chef who lived across the street. The only decision left to decide was what to wear.

"It's *my* birthday," Tina proclaimed. "I want the sparkly blue top, and I should get it."

Her bedroom was a mess, with clothes strewn all over the bed, chairs, and floor. She and Lenita had been trying on outfits for more than an hour. Because they exchanged clothes so often, neither was sure who owned what. Every time they went out together, a negotiation ensued.

"Ok, fine," Lenita relented. "But I get the red bell-bottom pants."

Before Tina could respond, Ms. Mae shouted from the front foyer, "Martina Jo, you got company. Y'all come on down here right now."

Puzzled, the girls crept to the top of the staircase and peeked over the rail.

"Girl, that's Big Jessie and JJ," Lenita said. "Did you know they were coming for your birthday?"

"Naw," Tina replied. "And who's that high-yellow thang talking to Momma? I know that ain't Shay, Ms. Marva's baby girl. If it is, she sho' ain't no baby no more."

At the tender age of 13, Natasha LaShay Morrison was anything but innocent. Short in stature, with toasted-tan skin and dark, waist-length curls, at a glance *Shay Baby* (her daddy's nickname) appeared no more remarkable than any of the many other half-white, half-black pre-teens prevalent in Midwest rural towns—but that was before you got close. Maybe it was the way she twirled her hair when she talked or how her blue-green eyes always seemed to direct your attention to her small but full cleavage, but there was little debate: Marva and Jessie's young, illegitimate offspring oozed sexuality.

Considering where and how she lived, one might expect Shay to *know* things. Since she'd been a toddler, she'd shared the dinner table with a bevy of "working girls" her father regularly entertained at their home. What was unexpected, especially by her mother, was how early Shay had learned to emulate, perfect, and then capitalize on the mannerisms the women portrayed. When the father-daughter relationship turned incestuous, no one argued with the notion that Big Jessie owned a hundred percent of the blame for the depravity. But apparently, it was Shay, not her father, who had initiated their first encounter. It happened when she was 11 years old, a few weeks removed from her first menstrual cycle. She'd been in the bathtub for nearly an hour, door slightly ajar, intently focused on her burgeoning mounds and curves. Maybe if her mother had been home—someone else to talk to—the scene might have played out differently. Or maybe not. Nature versus nurture.

"Daddy, come here quick! I need to show you something," Shay had screamed, scaring her tipsy father half to death.

As Big Jessie pushed through the door, his baby girl rose from the water like a burlesque dancer, soap-slicked breasts and peach-fuzz pubic hair in full view.

"Come look! I got a weird little mole on my thigh just like Momma's," the woman-child cooed seductively.

Shay stretched out her hand. Her father hesitated, a brief flash of conscience dulling his usual easy grin, and then closed the door.

The next day, when Shay awoke to find five crisp $20 bills arranged neatly atop her fuzzy pink Care Bears pillow, the die was cast. Adults say this simple gesture marked the origin of her father's sexual manipulation, but in Shay's mind, *she* was now in charge. Big Jessie never forced her. She decided whom she wanted to do it with: first her father and eventually other men. The financial perks were more than a girl her age could spend. Shay knew Big Jessie took a cut off the top, but she didn't care. Truth be told, her greatest reward was how she felt each time she enticed, seduced, and ultimately corrupted grown men: Shay felt *powerful.*

When her father asked her to accompany him to Kansas City to "teach her older sister what's what," it was *game on.*

SIX

Little Girls Lost

THE CROWD THAT HAD GATHERED in Ms. Mae's foyer was downright festive; that is, until Tina and Lenita stepped into full view. As they descended the narrow staircase, all conversation ceased.

"What 'chu waitin' for, chile?" Ms. Mae coaxed, wiping her dishwater-soaked hands on her dress. "Yo' daddy, brother, and sister came all the way from Topeka to take you shopping for your birthday. The least you can do is say hi."

Tina smiled stiffly and greeted everyone with a half-hug. While she and JJ had gone to the movies together just last Christmas, it had been nearly 10 years since she had laid eyes on her father...or Shay. Suddenly feeling out of place, Lenita dropped a quick "hi, y'all" and followed Ms. Mae into the kitchen.

"Girl, you sho' filled out," Big Jessie gushed, lecherously inspecting his daughter inch by inch. "You. Are. Beautiful."

As family reunions go, that first birthday visit was relatively uneventful. While JJ stayed at Ms. Mae's to hang with old friends, Big Jessie took Shay and Tina for pizza at the mall food court, doled out two wads of cash, and then retreated to the car. In no time flat, the girls had burned through more than three hundred dollars each at Macy's, Claire's, and the trendy Baker's Shoe Store. The whole time, Shay talked constantly about Topeka, how much fun it was to live there, and how generous her daddy was. Though the constant chatter was annoying, Tina couldn't help but be intrigued.

"You think I'm lying?" Shay asked. "Come visit on the weekend. You'll see."

And so it began. Every other weekend for the next four months, Big Jessie would show up on Friday, slip Ms. Mae a few hundred dollars (for what, exactly, no one knew), and drive back to Topeka with Tina, reportedly to spend time with her brother and sister. Tina would return home late on Sunday, weighed down with packages: clothes, jewelry, electronics, and anything else a teenager might desire.

At first, Tina was so excited when she got home that she couldn't wait to call Lenita to show off the newest trinket and drop the 4-1-1 on Shay and all the crazy goings-on at her daddy's house.

"She's fun to be around," Tina would admit, "but that little girl is so *fast*. And that house, wow! Nita, they do drugs all the time. They think I don't see, but I do. Daddy brings people home every night, lots of 'em—mostly sleazy women. Ms. Marva don't say nothin'. Sometimes I see 'em watching me and Shay, and it gives me the creeps. I try to stay out of the way."

A few trips in, Tina's mood shifted. No matter how many gifts she received, she didn't seem happy. There were no more excited phone calls, and eventually she stopped talking about the weekends altogether.

The drama finally came to a head one Friday night in late fall. As usual, Big Jessie and Shay showed up at Ms. Mae's just after dinner, only to find that Tina had vanished. In hindsight, everyone should have known something was awry. All week, Tina had been hinting that she might not *feel like* going to Topeka that weekend, but no one took her seriously—just moody teenage drama queen antics, her mother thought. Well, lesson learned.

Big Jessie stayed in town a full day and a half, waiting for his wayward child to return. By Sunday morning, when the search had turned up nothing, he hit the road, furious. A few hours later, Ms. Dana found Tina wrapped in an old Malibu Barbie blanket behind some luggage in her basement, crying her eyes out. She'd been there all along, hiding during the day, sneaking upstairs for bathroom and food breaks at night when everyone was asleep.

With a little coaxing, Ms. Dana was able to ferret out the horrifying explanation for her niece's uncharacteristically deviant behavior. Big Jessie wasn't only sexually abusing Tina; he was "teaching both his daughters how to make money" by renting them out to the highest bidders.

The revelation exploded across the family like a hand grenade. Ms. Mae went on a crying, cussing rampage, vacillating between guilt for her daughter's pain and rage at her estranged husband's depravity. Shay and JJ stayed in Topeka with Ms. Marva, but that Friday was the last time anyone saw Big Jessie Cole. Some say he skipped town when he found out his ex-wife had alerted the authorities. Others swore Ms. Mae's older brother, Buddy, a concrete mason who supplied staff, equipment, and materials for hundreds of construction projects across the state, had something to do with his sudden disappearance

Whatever the case, Tina was safe now. Unfortunately, the damage to her psyche had already been done.

SEVEN

Her Own Eyes

"HEY D, YOU HERE TO JOIN THE FUN?" Tina teased as Junkie #2 absent-mindedly caressed what used to be her firm, round behind.

Stunned into silence, Dana rested her backside against the porch railing and meticulously inspected the stranger standing in front of her. Tina was wearing cut-off denim shorts that exposed maximum butt cheeks and a too-large tank top missing its right shoulder strap. Technically, the girl was topless, her once-perfect breasts replaced by two dangling flesh sacks that situated her cracked nipples just above her waistline. Her eyes were a ghostly gray color, her hair brittle and sparse.

"If you want to score, you'd better get in there. Terran just cashed his check, and the hoes are all over him. That door sticks. You have to jiggle it."

This is not happening, Dana's mind protested. As if it were normal, had her strung-out cousin just announced that her husband was in a crack house when he should be at work? And how did Tina know Terran had gotten paid?

With no hint of acknowledgment, Dana jerked the dusty glass knob, slammed her full weight against the door, and forced her way inside. As she crossed the threshold into what appeared to be a makeshift boudoir, fear engulfed her. The room was unlit and reeked of smoke and sweat. Along the walls, Dana counted six or seven half-naked bodies. Some looked dead; others were twisted together, swaying to a sleepy jazz tune. If intercourse was happening, there was nothing romantic about it.

As her eyes adjusted to the darkness, her fear turned to disbelief. Seated in the corner furthest from the door was Terran, head back, eyes closed, half-clothed in his work uniform. He was perched on an old wicker throne adorned with dirty, colorful throws. His shirt was open, and his thick leather belt and black Dickie slacks were bunched around his ankles. Above him stood a tall, wild-haired brunette holding a joint the size of a fat cigar to his parched lips. On her knees directly in front of Terran was another woman—a girl, actually. Painfully skinny, so black she looked blue, this waif was butt-naked except for a pair of thigh-high red leather boots. As if hypnotized, Dana could not look away as the woman-child's head bobbed up and down in her husband's lap. She felt both sick to her stomach and sorry for the girl: this was obviously a sexual favor performed out of desperation.

What Dana did next would haunt her for months. Maybe it was shock or egotistically motivated embarrassment, but instead of yelling, cursing, or walking right up to Terran and bitch-slapping him across the face, she squeezed her eyes shut and quietly backed out of the room, through the garbage-filled kitchen, and out the back door. Then she ran.

By now, the sun was high in the sky, Benton Boulevard traffic was heavy, and the bus stop was packed. For Dana, none of this registered. She was too preoccupied with the sordid scenes flashing through her mind like snapshots from a camera. *Click!* Tina's bloodshot, gray eyes. *Click, click!* Red leather boots. *Click, click, click!* The Harley-Davidson belt buckle she'd given Terran for his 25th birthday, glistening against the stained wood floor.

How could she have been so stupid? Like a brain-dead Stepford wife, she'd missed all the cues. She and her husband had discussed the scenario a hundred times. Years ago on their first official date as husband and wife, they'd shared a joint at his friend Jeff's barbecue. That night, they'd agreed: a little weed was fine, but nothing harder.

"If you feel tempted," Dana had counseled. "Think of all the family and friends we've lost to the streets—and the morgue."

A horn blast from an angry delivery truck driver snapped Dana back to reality. She had been standing frozen in the middle of the street.

"You asshole! We talked about this!" Dana shouted, not concerned about who heard.

Suddenly exhausted, she crossed the intersection and headed for home.

Now what? She had to leave, didn't she? Take the boys away before he could drag them down with him. But this was Terran's mess. Why should she give up her home? *He* should be the one to go.

But her husband had always been proud and hard-headed, even before the drugs. What if he wouldn't leave? Trying not to panic, Dana picked up the pace. As she entered her kitchen through the back door—no lights, no neighbor's prying eyes—she decided: *Now is not the time to lose control.* Sure, she was devastated, but she would NOT fall apart. Not yet. She would wait until she could confront Terran and look him in the eye. Only then would she decide what was next.

EIGHT

Wake Up

"OH, MY HEAD."

Terran opened his eyes slowly, struggling to focus. *Damn. Not again.*

This wasn't supposed to happen. Sure, he'd made a conscious decision to take the detour, but only to score a quick pick-me-up to get through what was about to be a tough workday. In and out, that had been the plan. The dust in Terran's hair and crusted drool on his cheek told a different story, as did the sliver of starry sky peeking through the trash-bag-covered windows. It was *late.* Apparently, Terran had slept all day and much of the night on the dirty crack house floor, two strangers lying naked on top of him. He felt like shit: head pounding, eyes burning, mouth dry as cotton. Even worse, he had missed inspections again. Frank, his red-bearded, ill-tempered supervisor at the Chase meatpacking plant, would be pissed.

Though Terran would never admit it, he enjoyed hosting monthly inspections for Chase's efficiency team. As lead equipment monitor, he relished the notion that these "experts" *needed* what he *knew*. Terran liked the power the role afforded, and he enjoyed the work. What's more, he was good at it, a star performer recognized for his experience, technical skills, and poise under pressure. But a few months ago, he had begun to dread those encounters, and for good reason.

One cold Friday during an otherwise uneventful staff meeting about overtime pay and healthier vending machine snacks, Frank had unveiled a new safety protocol that would forever change the happy-go-lucky culture on the shop floor: random drug testing. Before, if a guy showed up to work hungover or sporting a hint of marijuana cologne, his line partner could discreetly step in and handle the heavy (translation: dangerous) assignments until the dude could pull himself together. The supervisor looked the other way, and the only repercussion was some good-natured ribbing. Since introducing the 24/7, 100% Clean program, or what the guys had affectionately re-named *the bum-rush*, this practice was no more.

Here's how it worked: inspectors would appear to be conducting a standard walk-through, asking questions, smiling in dudes' faces, shaking hands, and taking notes. When someone acted fidgety or suspiciously slipped away from the line for an unscheduled "break," the inspectors would leave, and five minutes later, the guy would be paged by human resources.

"Come on in. How's your day? No, nothing's wrong. Strictly routine, but yeah, we need you to pee in the cup..."

It happened just last week to Dak Martin, a quiet, 40-something welder and casual cokehead who worked the late shift. Less than two hours after he was paged, his partner had spotted two guards cleaning out his locker just as A-shift, Terran's crew, was punching in, no explanation—not that anyone needed one.

Whatever, Terran mentally assured himself. *I'm not Dak. I'm not a damn addict!*

But ever since last Christmas Eve when his friend Jay had convinced him to sprinkle a little white powder on a joint, Terran had feared he might be losing control. Why couldn't he get to work on time anymore? And why were his pockets always empty? No matter how well he planned, lately, he couldn't even scrape together a few bucks for an after-work drink with the guys. And yesterday he'd had to pawn his old scooter just to pay the rent. Well, *part* of the rent. If he hadn't held out some cash, he wouldn't have been able to take the detour that had landed him here today.

Ugh, today...

Embarrassed, Terran decoupled himself from his floormates, scooped up his slacks and underwear (he was still wearing his shirt, jacket, socks, and shoes), and ducked behind a ragged curtain that concealed a makeshift toilet in the house's only working bathroom. As he fastened his belt, Terran glimpsed his reflection in the rusty metal medicine cabinet; he hardly recognized his own face. His appearance was alarming—bloodshot eyes, cracked lips, and matted hair. Of more concern, though, was the sense of impending doom that he could not shake. In the past four years, he'd landed a steady job, married his best friend, rented a sweet house, and welcomed into the world his second healthy baby boy. As he fixed his gaze on the thousand-year-old wallpaper, he couldn't help but wonder if everything he'd always wanted was now teetering on the edge of a cliff.

Terran pulled the chain to flush (he still had some dignity) and then quietly slipped out to his car. Suddenly the little blue "it's definitely a boy" toy racecar spoke to him.

Wait a minute. He paused. *Dana?*

The memories burst forth in a flash—his wife staring, disgust in her eyes, the beet-red flocking on the crack house walls taunting him.

Had he been dreaming, or had Dana been there?

NINE

Altered State

D ANA HAD ENTERED HER BACK DOOR like a thief, spilling the contents of her purse as she let it drop to the floor. There was no way she could go next door to get the boys—not like this. The look in her eyes would scare them to death. Like a zombie, she made her way to the living room couch, a single tear beginning to form in the corner of one eye. Ten minutes later, the doorbell rang.

Malia, she cursed. *Damn, that girl has some kind of radar.*

"Hey," Dana mumbled, trying to sound sleepy as she robotically opened the door.

"Hey." Malia barged in, dropped her keys on the coffee table, and made a beeline to the fridge for orange juice.

"Don't pass out. I was up, so I thought I'd come on over and save you a bus ride. But girl, you better not be late picking me up. And don't use up all my gas. Are the boys up yet? I can't believe Tyler's not yelling at the top of his lungs right now."

As she closed the refrigerator door and their eyes met, Malia suddenly stopped talking.

"What's wrong with you?" she asked. "Why you already dressed? I didn't know you knew how to get up this early. And what's with the hair? Eek."

Before Dana could come up with one of her snarky comebacks, Malia was up the stairs, pushing through the door of the boys' room.

"Where are my nephews? Did you finally kick them out of the house for being so crazy?" Malia joked.

For the first time since witnessing the freak show at the crack house, Dana smiled.

"Naw, not my beautiful babies. They're at the neighbors'. I told you I have stuff to do."

Satisfied, Malia headed for the door, pulling Dana with her. "Well, since you're ready, let's go," she said. "Miracle of miracles, I might get to work on time."

Throughout the 20-minute ride downtown to the Missouri Division of Family Services' central office, the chatter was definitely one-sided. Malia rattled on about her latest workplace annoyance, unaware that Dana was unusually quiet.

While social work was definitely in her blood (more on that later), cleaning up drama wasn't the first career choice anyone expected Malia to pursue. True, she always seemed to have the 4-1-1 on family goings-on. But when real conflict arose between sisters, cousins, and the like, of all the Lawton girls, Malia would be the one voted most likely to run the other way. Besides, by the end of middle school, everyone knew she had already adopted what she considered a foolproof plan for a perfect life: graduate high school with honors, pursue a communications degree, probably in journalism, land a prestigious job at a Fortune 500 company, get married, and live happily ever after.

"Just like 'my sister, Lenita,'" her college friends often teased.

Malia did earn the degree, but after only two years of writing uninspired copy for the local black newspaper, she set out to chart her own course. Her path was revealed the following summer as she was interviewing a local community advocate for an expose about the wives and children of PTSD-plagued veterans. The article sparked controversy across state and local government, capturing the attention of the new DFS director. Six months later, she had left the newspaper, completed paralegal courses, and accepted an unsolicited job offer as a family counselor—a role that paired her love of children with her insatiable desire to get all up in other people's business.

Fate, her sisters had concluded. *History repeating itself.*

In the mid-1950s, Momma Dana, the third of six siblings, had been one of only a handful of black students to earn an associate's degree in social work from the city's nearly all-white community college. The senior Dana had then spent more than 15 years advocating for poor single mothers and their children. As far as the family was concerned, mouthy, opinionated Malia, defender of mischievous toddlers near and far, was exactly where God wanted her to be.

Though Malia drove her nuts, Dana truly admired her sister. Malia was a dedicated professional who genuinely cared about her clients and their children. That said, no humans on the planet were more central to Malia's existence than TJ, Tyler, and her other nieces and nephews. She reminded Dana of that fact as she pulled into short-term parking.

"I better get in there," she said. "Be sure to bring the boys when you come back. They need to see me."

She climbed out of the car and watched Dana drag herself over to the driver's seat. As she watched her baby sister settle in behind the wheel, Malia leaned in and looked deep into her eyes.

"You sick?" she asked suspiciously. "You seem sick to me."

"Thanks for the car. I'll call you later," Dana mumbled as she drove away.

The drive home was downright ghostly—no sounds, no traffic, just the same disturbing images flashing through Dana's mind. By the time she turned onto her block, the world was wide awake. It was nearly 8:00 a.m. As she drew closer to her house, she could see TJ in the neighbor's yard, trying to teach Tyler to catch a half-deflated basketball. To his annoyance, his baby brother—

preoccupied with the spiky blades of grass between his chubby toes—was *so* not interested.

Dana waved to the kids and held up an index finger for Nae—the universal sign for "one minute." She pulled into the driveway a little too close to the bushes, rushed in the back door, and fell to the floor. What had Malia just said about her looking sick?

Dana had been experiencing so much lately—confusion, shock, rage, depression—it was no wonder she'd missed some physical cues. Between Terran's bizarre outbursts and the money problems, she'd been an emotional wreck. Then there had been the awful scene that morning. Well, Dana was paying attention now. Her eyes were swollen and red, which made sense since she wasn't sleeping, but her stomach also hurt. Not pain, exactly…more of a dull ache pulling on her abdomen. And lately she'd been itching "down there." Add the fact that she was exhausted all the time, and maybe Malia was on to something.

Okay. Doctor's appointment. That was something Dana *could* control.

TEN

The End of Innocence

Damn. A sister trying her best to do right and wrong still wins. I hear you, Dana: what the hell is the point?

♥

VENEREAL DISEASE. VD. The clap. In line at the pharmacy, Dana's mind was racing. Why this, why her, why now? She had been "fast" as a teenager, but she had always prided herself on having only one boyfriend at a time. And she'd only had sex with boys she trusted.

What a joke! If it wasn't for her husband, the person she trusted more than anyone in her life, she wouldn't be standing here, listening to some 12-year-old warn her about the risks of PID and infertility if she didn't take all the antibiotics, even after she felt better. Mortified, she tried her best not to make eye contact. Soon embarrassment turned to sadness, sadness to depression. Ultimately, depression gave way to rage.

What was it Momma always told her?

"Baby, if you want to be happy, do right, even when others do wrong. Be a good girl. Love your man even when he doesn't deserve it. Put your kids first."

Nice dream, Dana scoffed. She had done all of that...and look where it had gotten her. Not yet 30 years old, a single parent for all intents and purposes, undergoing medical treatment for a horny teenager's disease, finances a mess, and her husband a bona fide crackhead whose life was now in danger...literally. Dana had seen how this story ended for good girls—they keep the faith no matter what, trying to be Superwoman by day, working themselves to death, running around town all night chasing their man, a screaming kid hanging on each leg. Then, one day, they wake up fat, old, and unattractive, realizing life has passed them by—no joy, no excitement—and ironically, no man.

Well, not Dana. She wasn't going out like that—she wouldn't leave. Terran and the boys were her everything, but she wouldn't be a victim, or take the blame for her husband's shortcomings. Dana knew she still had "it." She could still turn heads. Lots of men found her attractive, even if Terran couldn't see it anymore. Hell, just the other day, a handsome dude with curly hair and kind eyes had followed her around the grocery store, flirting. When they'd reached the register, he'd even paid her bill and practically begged her to call him if she needed a shopping buddy again.

Dana paid the sleepy-eyed pharmacist and ran out the door. She climbed into the car, pausing before putting the key in the ignition to search her purse for that grocery receipt with the name and number scribbled on the back. *Mike.* That was his name.

For the first time in days, Dana actually felt like smiling. *Maybe it's time I live a little.*

ELEVEN

A New Normal

"I SAID I GOT THIS. NOW BACK OFF."

That was Terran's response. No remorse. No apology. This man had just destroyed her life, and potentially the lives of her children, and all he had to offer was macho bullshit.

Dana lay half passed out in the colorful awning on her back porch, downing Tequila shots as her children napped on the woven rug at her feet, staring at nothing, struggling to make sense of the madness.

The confrontation with her husband had been brief but intense. What had started as whisper-fighting—the kind of arguing parents of toddlers often engage in—soon escalated into full-out war. For a moment, when Terran, all smiles, had burst onto the scene, scooped up TJ, and asked, "What we eatin'?" Dana had seriously considered whether she had dreamed the entire thing. *If only.*

Dana was at the stove, stirring spaghetti sauce, her back to the door. At the sound of her husband's voice, she halted, shifted Tyler from one hip to the other, and leaned against the wall to steady herself.

"How was work?" she said, her words dripping with sarcasm.

"You know, same old shit," Terran replied without making eye contact.

"*You* tired?" she continued, a little louder than the situation called for. "Seems more like wired to me."

Now Terran was on the kitchen floor, playing race cars with his sons. A change in his wife's tone prompted him to look up. There was no mistaking it; she was *pissed.* And this was not the heart-wrenching, "you hurt my feelings" kind of anger. Her eyes were red, but he was sure she had *not* been crying. Hand on hip, head cocked to the side, lips pursed... *If looks could kill,* Terran observed, *I'd be pushing up daisies.*

On autopilot, Terran did what he always did when he knew whatever was wrong was probably his fault. He deflected.

"Why you trippin'? I'm the one who should be mad," Terran replied. "You left the car on 'E' again. I had to stop for gas, which made me late for work. If I lose my job, then where y'all gon' live? What you need to do is chill."

Dana stared at Terran for what seemed like an eternity. Then, like a robot, she took TJ by the hand and quietly escorted the boys upstairs.

"Honey," she told her oldest, "you and your brother gon' watch the Ninja Turtles video while Daddy and I have a talk," forcing a smile that didn't reach her eyes.

She put Tyler on the floor of the bedroom and shoved the tape into the VCR. Intuitively TJ plopped down beside his baby brother without saying a word. Dana closed the door and headed back downstairs.

By now, Terran had turned the heat off under the sauce. As he reached into the refrigerator to grab a beer, Dana reached out and slammed it shut, nearly crushing his fingers.

"I *saw* you!" she screamed. "I saw it all!"

Once she began, the words poured out like a raging river. She walked Terran through her entire horrific day, recounting in excruciating detail how she had followed him, thinking he might be having an affair. She tried unsuccessfully to describe the inexplicable force that had compelled her to turn right, towards the crack house, instead of left, to the bus stop. She even shared the disgusting Tina sighting, the horrible scene in the crack house living room, the gonorrhea diagnosis, everything.

As she yelled insults, calling her husband a crackhead, a junkie, an unfit father, threatening to turn him in to the authorities or kick him out of the house, Terran sat quietly at the kitchen table, staring at his hands. Sadly, he had dreaded this day ever since the night he'd traded his son's PlayStation for a rock. His head had repeatedly told him he had a problem; his ego wouldn't listen.

As the tirade subsided, with words like "asshole," "man-whore," and "traitor" spilling from Dana's tightly pursed lips between long pauses, Terran suddenly leaped from his chair and slammed his fists on the already-unsteady glass top.

"You done?" he growled through gritted teeth. "Cuz now *I* got something to say. Yeah, this is messed up, especially the VD, but it's not *all* my fault. You put so much pressure on me—you and the kids always needing stuff. Well, I need stuff, too. So I do drugs sometimes, but I ain't no junkie. I got this. If you don't like it, you can leave. This is my house."

And with that, the gauntlet was thrown.

TWELVE

Great Performances

IT HAD BEEN NEARLY THREE WEEKS since Terran's big
revelation, or, as Dana described it, "the day all the shit hit the
fan." But from what family and friends could see, nothing had
changed. Terran's machismo and Dana's "ain't nobody gonna
break up my family" defiance had transformed the pair into
Academy Award-winning actors. The fake-happy couple still sat
next to each other during Momma D's Sunday dinners, a fidgety
kid on each lap. Same ol', same ol': a houseful of sisters, brothers,
cousins, neighbors...mismatched plates overflowing with fried
chicken, sweet potatoes, and collard greens...TJ and Tyler being
passed from one set of loving hands to another with nobody the
wiser.

At home, the performances were more like one-act plays. Now that his secret was out, Terran no longer even pretended to do right. He would disappear for days, returning only to shower and change clothes. On the few evenings the couple was at home together, Dana busied herself in the kitchen, hoping to shield her babies from the alternating flashes of pain and rage in her eyes as she watched her sons engage in the always-epic wrestling matches with the father they adored. Whether or not Terran was present, every night at dinnertime, Dana would use the same playful words to call the boys to the kitchen to wash their hands.

"Time to chop off those grubby little fingers!" she'd yell.

Sometimes Terran joined them and took charge of the handwashing. If Dana chose to leave the room—act one over—he would even say grace before coaxing the boys into finishing their meals by threatening to steal food from their plates. More often, the call to eat served as the perfect distraction for Terran to slip out the back door. TJ and Tyler rarely noticed, but if eyes were knives, Terran would have been cut to shreds by the daggers Dana threw his way.

Project perfection at all costs: that was the unspoken agreement. But like all performances, eventually the curtain *must* come down.

THIRTEEN

Stalker

"HEY, LOW-FAT CHOCOLATE MILK, is that you?"

It had been nearly a month since their playful encounter, but Dana recognized his voice immediately. She tried not to smile.

"So, what's up? You still hanging around the dairy aisle, trying to pick up women?" she said, turning around just in time to see him blush.

"Not just any women." Mike winked.

He was just as cute as she remembered. Tall, caramel brown, older than her...but not *old*. Same sexy smile and kind eyes. The two officially introduced themselves and then strolled casually from aisle to aisle, filling their carts and making small talk about which breakfast cereal tastes best after a night of partying. Dana couldn't help but reminisce. Before TJ was born, *this* had been her life. Sassy, confident, free. If she found someone attractive, all she had to do was make eye contact…and it was on. Sometimes the encounter ended with nothing more than a casual flirtation, but if the mood was right, "single Dana" wouldn't think twice about going all the way, including a little afternoon delight. As she watched her handsome shopping buddy pick out the perfect cucumber, she wondered. Given what *wasn't* happening in the Jackson bedroom these days, would anyone blame her for falling back into old habits?

Since the boys weren't with her (TJ and Tyler had spent the night with their cousin Alex, Nita's four-year-old son), Dana was in no hurry to get home. When they reached the checkout line, the conversation showed no signs of waning. Dana insisted Mike pay for his groceries first—she wasn't about to take his money again. He was sweet, but in her experience, men who pay have expectations.

After checkout, the duo proceeded to the parking lot, carts side by side. Suddenly the conversation took a more personal turn.

"So, if I haven't made it clear already, I am single," Mike said, accepting Dana's grocery bags and loading them into her trunk as if they shared mundane tasks like this every day.

"That ring on your finger says 'married,' but I have yet to hear any mention of a husband. Why is that?"

Dana closed the trunk and made her way around to her driver-side door. Mike's navy-blue Chevy pickup sat one space away. *Serendipity.* After unloading his groceries, Mike dutifully delivered both carts to the return station, slipped his keys into his pocket, and sidled up next to Dana, all smiles: he definitely was NOT ready to leave. As their elbows touched, something in Dana just snapped. Before she could stop herself, she was telling this man everything: how, in the blink of an eye, she and Terran had gone from married bliss to total chaos. Through stored-up tears, she detailed the awful scene in which she had discovered Terran was on crack cocaine, the venereal disease, their epic fights, and how they were now living in limbo, putting on airs for the sake of the children. If Mike was repulsed or in the least bit taken aback, he never let on. He listened, completing her sentences now and then as if reading her mind. By the time the tears subsided, they were leaning on the hood of Mike's truck, looking away from each other, not touching physically, but closer than two almost-complete strangers could have ever imagined.

After a few moments of silence, Mike cautiously took hold of Dana's trembling hands.

"I'm so sorry this is happening to you," he started. "No one deserves such pain. But God forgive me, I'm also *so* grateful. You couldn't have known this, but *your* story is *my* story, first with my baby sister and then 15 years ago with my wife. My sister died. My wife vanished. I've never talked about this to anyone until today. Dana, you set me free."

For most people, this heartfelt revelation would have ended in a litany of tender affirmations and warm platitudes. But Dana wasn't most people. Mike's unexpected vulnerability touched her, but given he hadn't said 10 words throughout the entire exchange, something told her going deeper would not be good for him—or her. Truth be told, she was spent—and a little embarrassed. Like flipping a switch, she cleared her throat, pulled her shoulders back, and ever so effortlessly tapped into the surefire Lawton family remedy for heavy emotional drama: sarcasm.

"Well, *that* was fun," she quipped, wiping her eyes with her sleeve. "Too bad I forgot to clip the free psychoanalysis coupon in this week's circular. It was right there next to 'Pork Chops, $2.99 a pound.' That's why I shop here. This store has *everything*."

Mike smiled and squeezed her hand.

"Yeah," he added, not missing a beat. "And their peaches are the freshest in the hood."

Mike and Dana looked up simultaneously and laughed out loud. Dana stood first, opening her arms, the universal invitation for a hug. After embracing for several seconds, Mike pulled away first, his hand lifting Dana's chin so he could see her eyes. Then he kissed her on the lips. The act was sweet, not passionate, like a precious gift. There was no mistaking that he found her attractive, but Mike was also keenly aware of how vulnerable she was right now. If he'd learned anything from his own disastrous experiences with drugs and family, the best thing he could do for this beautiful, tortured soul was to give her space.

When he opened his eyes, Dana's face was a cross between a smile and a smirk. In an instant, they both knew the "will we, won't we" question had been answered. If they saw each other again, they would meet as friends. They'd flirt, but nothing more. No lustful secrets. No tawdry affair. What had happened that crisp morning in the Happy Eats grocery store parking lot was worth so much more than casual sexual release. Dana and Mike had shared a connection.

Mike reached around Dana's waist to open her car door.

"This was priceless," he said. "Unforgettable. But there's one more thing I *must* say. Please be careful. And I'm not talking about the obvious risks of living with an addict: stuff like losing your home or the ever-present threat of physical violence. I'm talking about losing your soul. My guess is I'm a lot older than you, but thanks to Master Crack, I'm sure I'm way behind in emotional stability. It took me a long time to get past the anger, then the guilt, and finally the shame. I went to a dark place, including a brief stint buried in my own addiction. Trust me when I say it's *so* easy to fall."

Dana nodded and started the engine, and instead of a verbal "goodbye," she playfully drummed her fingers atop Mike's strong, warm hands. As she pulled out of the parking lot, she thought about how deeply she despised everything about illicit drugs. The chances of her *falling*, of becoming a user, seemed about as likely as her becoming ringleader for the Barnum & Bailey Circus.

That was then.

FOURTEEN

A Fatal Experiment

I see you, D. Nothing like a little flirtation to reclaim your dignity. Now what'chu gonna do with all that power?

♥

WHAT'S MOST EXTRAORDINARY is how... well ... ordinary the day was. It was Saturday, 5:00 a.m., early or late, depending on your perspective. The kids were still asleep, and as was the case those days, Dana lay in bed alone, no Terran, staring at the water-stained ceiling above her queen-sized. Some mornings, TJ would discover his dad passed out on the couch on his way to get some "good water" from the refrigerator dispenser. But more often than not, the green and blue sofa pillows remained just as undisturbed as the neatly tucked comforter on the left side of Dana's bed. The first few times Terran stayed out all night, Dana had been concerned. This man had betrayed her in more ways than she could count, but he was still her husband and the father of her children. Once, she had even called the police.

"If you don't hear from him in a day or two, call us back," the emotionless voice had instructed.

The next morning, after Terran casually strolled in the back door, grabbed a beer from the refrigerator, and headed to the shower with not so much as a "hello," Dana willed herself to stop caring.

Conceding that sleep was over, Dana dragged herself out of bed and began peeling the sheets from the mattress. Today was laundry day, the best day of the week if you asked her boys. Dana tossed the linen into the overflowing hamper at the foot of the bed and contemplated the rest of her day.

The Wash House laundromat was only about six blocks away, a brief walk through the park, past the basketball court and rickety old swings, next door to Mr. Jamison's ice cream shop. Open 24 hours a day, except Sunday, the place was always alive with sound: the whir of industrial-strength clothes dryers well past their expiration date, 70s dance music blaring from crackly wall speakers, and kids…screaming, laughing little bundles of energy everywhere you turned. No judgment, though, since no one had money for a babysitter. Single Mothers Central, the men in the neighborhood called it.

"I'm a big boy," TJ would proclaim as Dana let him believe he was pulling his brother in the clothes-filled Radio Flyer wagon all by himself.

Once there, "Let me do it," the boys would beg, fighting over whose turn it was to add the fabric softener. If her Irish twins maintained some semblance of control through the three-plus hours of cleaning, fluffing, and folding, Dana would reward their good behavior with chocolate and vanilla soft-serve with sprinkles.

Dana peered under the bed in search of hidden underwear and weighed the pros and cons. The walk through the park, other kids to play with, and the treats afterward would bring her children so much joy, but in her current headspace, she wasn't sure she could take it: the depressing incandescent lights, the incompatible aromas of Clorox and marijuana in the air, and, above all, the mindless chatter of disgruntled want-to-be ghetto wives droning on about their pregnant teenagers, overdue rent, and cheating boyfriends. Ugh. A better plan might be to commandeer Lenita's washer and dryer. The boys would be just as content playing kickball in the backyard with Alex. And who knows? Maybe she'd finally muster up enough courage to talk things through with her sister.

On the way to the bathroom, Dana kneeled down to extract a dirty sock from one of Terran's work boots. As she tossed the muddy footwear into the closet, annoyed that his clean clothes still mattered to her, something metallic caught her eye.

Uh-uh. I know this idiot didn't bring a gun into my home, around my children. On all fours, Dana cautiously looped her thumb and forefinger around what felt like a steel handle. The object was small and slender, about the length of her hand, partially wrapped in a faded blue towel dotted with soot. *Gun, my ass! That is a crack pipe.* Shocked, she fell back against the wall to study this weapon of mass destruction. This pipe wasn't like those used by the junkies at the bus stop; it was much fancier, with a thick, Pyrex-like glass cylinder, rubber-coated metal bolts connecting two sections of the shank, and a psychedelic painted bulb at the end. Inside the bulb were two white/yellow crystals.

"What the fuck?!" she whispered, thinking of the boys asleep across the hall.

Tossing the towel aside, her first thought was to go to the backyard, grab a hammer, and smash her discovery into a million pieces. *That would teach Terran a lesson…* But the longer Dana held the pipe, the more curious she became. She hid the tool under her oversized sleep shirt and tiptoed into the bathroom. Next she placed the pipe on the vanity, lit a vanilla-scented candle, and opened the window. Robotically, she locked the door, sat down on the side of the tub, and buried her face in her hands. *Enough!*

For months now, she had felt like she was suffocating, trapped in a life she did not recognize. It was as if she was looking up at the world from a deep hole. As she contemplated her next move, vivid images of crack-addicted friends trolling the streets like zombies flooded her psyche. But Dana didn't care. Right now, she needed a break. Plus, maybe if she tried this drug, just this once, she might better understand its power. Besides, she was a devout cheapskate. Even if she enjoyed the experience, she reasoned, there would be *no way* she could get addicted.

Once she decided, doing the deed was easy. Months before, at a party, Dana had watched her cousin Tina smoke crack. Holding the pipe at a connector so as not to burn her fingers, Dana flicked on the green Bic lighter she kept in the vanity and waved the flame beneath the bulb. Watching the crystal rocks crackle and dissolve, she took a few deep breaths. Like an experienced professional, she gently placed her lips on the mouthpiece and inhaled the translucent clouds of dense white smoke. Dana then exhaled slowly, sending smoke billowing up and out the window.

At first, she felt nothing. Doubting her technique, she heated the bulb again and took another hit. This time, she angled the pipe upward, threw her head back, closed her eyes, and held her breath until she felt as if she'd pass out. The high started as a tingling in her feet, and then a fluttering up her legs like deranged butterflies. Soon her entire body was buzzing in a purely sensual way, like the sensation immediately before orgasm. When she finally exhaled, the room shook. Her ears itched, and somewhere in the distance, bells rang. With subsequent hits, the sensations reoccurred, though with less intensity. For the first time in an eternity, she felt happy, invincible.

After 20 minutes or so, the feeling subsided, and Dana found herself sitting on the cold tile floor, staring at the black soot that had replaced the magic stones. The sadness she'd felt earlier had returned with a vengeance, but she also felt hope: she had discovered a way to ease the pain, at least temporarily.

No question, she vowed. *I will be doing that again.*

Crackhead 101

To crack virgins and to the sanctimoniously judgmental among us, at this point in the story, it feels appropriate to drop some knowledge about why this drug is so difficult to quit. Minds open.

♥

ACCORDING TO A RECENT ARTICLE on *psychcentral.com,* it is a mistake to believe those who abuse drugs simply lack willpower or moral principles.[1] In reality, drug addiction is a complex disease for which a cure requires much more than good intentions. Doctors have found addictive drugs actually change the brain by flooding the *nucleus accumbens,* the area most closely associated with motivation, reward, and survival, with the chemical messenger *dopamine*. These artificially induced surges of dopamine produce intense feelings of euphoria, compelling the user to repeat the unhealthy behavior again and again. Over time, the brain adapts by reducing the ability of the brain's reward system to respond appropriately: users must take more of the drug just to achieve the same "high." Eventually, without stimulus, the user finds it difficult to derive pleasure from anything—food, sex, or other social activities he or she once enjoyed. Despite being fully aware of the devastating impact their behavior is having on themselves and others, the addict continues to indulge. At this point, shutting the user out and leaving him to his own self-destructive devices might be the worst thing a loved one can do.

While the National Institutes of Health (NIH) can't specifically track crack overdoses, the agency recently reported a rise in the number of fatal overdoses related to overall cocaine use. According to a March 2018 *CDC* Morbidity and Mortality Report, between 1999 and 2015 in the United States, nearly 570,000 people died from drug overdoses. From 2015 to 2016, deaths increased across all the drug categories examined. The largest overall rate of increases occurred among deaths involving cocaine

(+52.4%) and synthetic opioids (+100%), most likely driven by illicitly manufactured Fentanyl.[2]

Another chronic public health issue related to crack cocaine is the spread of disease. Heavy crack smokers often transmit HIV, hepatitis C, and other deadly viruses when they burn or cut their lips and then share broken and makeshift pipes.

Unfortunately, to a committed addict, these cold, hard facts are little more than noise.

FIFTEEN

Malia Don't Play

"Y'ALL GETTIN' SO BIG."

Whirlwind Malia strikes again. The intrusion annoyed Dana, but it did not surprise her. It had been over six weeks since the sisters had laid eyes on each other. They'd talked on the phone, but each time Malia suggested a visit, Dana would manufacture an excuse: the boys weren't home—they were spending the night with Terran's sister—the house was being fumigated, or Dana had to babysit the neighbor's cat. For Malia, who hadn't been away from her nephews for more than three weeks since Tyler had been born, this would *not* do.

I knew I would eventually have to face her, Dana thought. *But dear God, why does it have to be today?* From the kitchen, she could hear her kids jumping up and down, water splashing, and a chair being pushed across the linoleum floor. She lifted the blanket just enough to watch her sister lay freshly washed bath towels on the counter and peel the cellophane from an unopened bottle of baby shampoo. While Dana practically had to hog-tie her boys to pour water on their heads, TJ and Tyler would stand at attention forever in anticipation of having their hair washed by their doting aunt.

"It's how I use the sprayer," Malia would explain. "It's kinda messy, but I treat it like a trip to the water park."

Tyler squealed as tiny shampoo bubbles trickled down his face and into his ears. Feeling left out, TJ dropped his Hot Wheels race cars on the slippery floor and wrapped his arms around his auntie's short legs.

"Is it my turn yet?" he pouted.

"Soon, big boy," Malia promised, careful not to lose her grip on Tyler's head. "Baby brother first, remember?"

To anyone else, the scene Malia had walked in on a few hours earlier would have appeared perfectly normal: an exhausted mother napping on the couch—after all, it *was* the weekend. The kids were disheveled but no worse for wear. Well, Malia wasn't *anyone*.

When she'd arrived unannounced on Dana's front porch, it had been foggy and not yet light outside. She'd knocked for at least five minutes, but Dana had pretended not to hear. Finally Malia had had enough.

"D, you know I can see you, right?" she had shouted through half-drawn curtains. "Stop playing and let me in."

Groaning, Dana had dragged herself up, disengaged the lock, and then sprinted back to the sofa and covered her head with the musty plaid blanket.

As soon as Malia entered, her smile disappeared. The house was a wreck. An overflowing laundry basket blocked the entrance to the kitchen, and stuffed animals littered the stairs. Dana had planted TJ and Tyler in front of the TV, shirtless and unwashed, eating Cracker Jack caramel corn and watching *Ren & Stimpy*, a deranged cartoon surely conceived by someone hyped up on a controlled substance stronger than anything Dana had ever encountered.

Without so much as a hello, Malia set about fixing things. She worked silently, whipping up a makeshift breakfast of grilled cheese and apple juice, washing dishes, vacuuming, and putting away toys. Through it all, Dana lay perfectly still, partly to evade her sister's wrath but mostly to avoid the excruciating pain that pierced her right temple every time she moved her head. Unfortunately, today was one of her more lucid days. Unlike previous mornings after, Dana felt *everything*. Her eyes burned, her arms and legs itched, and her head felt as if it was being pulled away from her body. Emotionally she was in hell. The most carefree girl in the Lawton family was nervous, furious even, for reasons she couldn't explain. Her chest felt so weighed down with sadness that it was difficult to breathe. As she counted the *stomp,*

stomp, stomp of her sister's footsteps on the hardwood floors, Dana couldn't recall the last time she been happy. Wait, she could. It was the day she'd found Terran's pipe.

That first morning after had been so different, in a good way. Sure, Dana had been a little bummed after she'd come down from her first crack high, but nothing so consequential as to derail her plans for the day. After disposing of the evidence (she'd found a new hiding place for the pipe), she had felt energized. She cleaned the entire house, but had decided to skip the laundry and take the boys to the park. When they got home, Dana could tell Terran had been there, probably to change clothes but also to retrieve his *property.* There were wet towels on the bathroom floor, and the couple's bedroom was a wreck: dresser drawers half-open, pillows on the floor, closets tossed.

Serves you right, Dana fumed.

Because she'd repeatedly threatened to call the police if she ever found a crumb of narcotics in her house, Dana knew Terran would never ask her about the missing tool.

Maybe if he had confronted her, things would have turned out differently.

Or maybe not.

SIXTEEN

Junkie In Training

YOU CAN'T GET HOOKED after one time. That's what Tina had said. *Yeah, right.*

It was Wednesday, four days after the pipe discovery. The boys were at the neighbors, "cuz sometimes Momma needs a break," TJ had explained to his brother.

Dana and Tina huddled together on the bus stop bench, surrounded by a group of cocky pubescent boys trying to look like men: faces blank, eyes darting back and forth, fingers wiggling nervously inside baggy pants pockets. Dana had called Tina about an hour ago, unable or unwilling to delay any longer. She was nervous, but her mind was made up. She wanted to cop, and given what she'd seen at the crack house, she was sure Tina could make that happen.

"If you're nervous," Tina coaxed, "we can start with a little one."
Nodding in agreement, Dana reached into her bra to produce a sweaty ten-dollar bill. She'd seen drug buys go down at that spot several times, but now that *she* was the customer, the process felt unfamiliar. She placed the bill on the seat next to her and, without making eye contact, said, "Gimme a dime," to no one in particular. On cue, the smallest of the crew plopped down beside her, eyes forward. Looking not a day over 15, the baby-faced entrepreneur swapped the cash for a one-inch Ziploc bag. Inside was a single jagged crystal rock about the size of a navy bean. Her heart racing and her palms sweating, Dana snatched up the package and rushed to Malia's borrowed car, with Tina stumbling to keep up.

For a blissful half-hour, the two took turns: prep, light up, smoke, repeat. As if in a trance, Dana made the 30-second trek back to the bus stop two, three, maybe four more times—she wasn't sure. Like the first time, the highs were mind-blowing. Electric! But after each crash, the lows were equally intense, as if someone had just thrown icy water on her soul. Before they knew it, she and Tina were leaning on the car's driver-side door staring into an empty wallet. In less than two hours, the whacked-out cousins had burned through $70—grocery money Terran had left on the dining room table, likely to prove he wasn't a complete asshole. Dana should have been freaking out, but she was too distracted, brainstorming schemes to get more money.

"I gotta go," she announced abruptly, leaving Tina standing in the parking lot alone, glassy-eyed and agitated.

From then on, the pattern was set. Each morning before dawn, Dana would drag her shrinking body out of bed, full of confidence. The first hours were relatively routine: tidy the house, breakfast for the boys (a cup of strong coffee for herself), and then an hour or so on the phone with Ms. Jackson from across the street to dissect the latest episode of *Days of Our Lives*.

At her husband's insistence, Dana hadn't officially worked outside the home since they'd married. But her husband's bravado hadn't kept her from picking up a side hustle now and then, from babysitting to braiding hair to cleaning house and running errands for her elderly neighbors. On days she was busy, Dana's resolve to abstain from using extended well past dinnertime. But no matter the distraction, the impulse to get high was ever-present. The only question was what would be the trigger? These days, a fussy baby, burnt toast, or even something as benign as a sad TV commercial could reduce her to tears, causing her to drop everything and run out to score. Eventually Dana would return to her frightened children (having Nae right next door was a godsend) and vow to never touch the stuff again. Inevitably, though, the itch would reemerge and the cycle would repeat.

Over the next three months, Dana would sell the microwave, pawn her wedding ring, shoplift, and even stand idly by as an old, crusty dealer felt her up in exchange for "credit." There was no denying she was flirting with disaster. But, she reasoned, since she always made sure her kids were safe, she couldn't be *that* far gone. In a weird way, Terran's disappearing acts helped to affirm the lie.

He was paying the most important bills, so the family still had a home with heat and running water. And since for several weeks, he had gone to great lengths to avoid being in the same room with Dana, Terran had yet to witness the alarming physical changes his once radiant, voluptuous bride was going through.

Steering clear of Malia, however, was something different entirely.

SEVENTEEN

A Reckoning

"GET UP RIGHT NOW or I'm callin' Momma," Malia demanded through gritted teeth. Judging by the dirty ring in the sink and how rapidly the little monsters had passed out on the living room floor, it had been a while since TJ and Tyler had experienced the relaxing water play of a kitchen shampoo.

Still buried beneath the blanket, Dana could feel her typically unrestrained older sister staring down at her. She pulled the cover more tightly around her body, a move that agitated Malia even more. With ninja-like swiftness, her sister snatched the blanket away and flipped Dana's feet to the floor.

"Really, D?" she said, louder than she'd planned. "You of all people *on that end?* I knew something was up, but I just thought you were tripping off Terran's mess. I'm not about to waste time

talking about how you got here; I just want to know how you gon'
fix it. Shit, girl! Have you looked in a mirror lately?"

Dana sat up without opening her eyes. Lately she'd been
avoiding mirrors, not at all interested in confirming what she
already knew to be true. Besides, the look on Malia's face was
reflective enough.

Since the last time the sisters were together, Dana had lost at
least 15 pounds. Her eyes were chronically bloodshot, her hair
thickly matted, and her teeth had turned a sickly brownish gray.
Although nothing fit, Malia noted, her sister's clothes were clean.
At least she's doing laundry.

The most alarming physical change was in the skin on Dana's
face and neck. Her once-perfect caramel-colored complexion was
now dotted with small white blisters the size of Rice Krispies. For
Malia, the pus-filled lesions brought to mind a wicked witch mask
from Halloweens past. Eventually the pimples would become
scabs, and the scabs would give way to irreversible skin rot.

"Okay, I give," Dana sighed. "Shit, Malia, don't you think I
know how fucked up this is? I'm pissed off. I'll even admit I might
be depressed. But I'm not *stupid.*"

With a burst of energy that surprised even her, Dana kicked
away the rest of the blanket and sprang to her feet, an action that
triggered a coughing fit the likes of which Malia had never seen.
Before her sister could freak out, Dana darted up the stairs to the
bathroom, her eyes watering and thick green phlegm spurting
from her mouth and nose. Malia froze, not sure which emotion to

acknowledge first—terror or rage. Thankfully, the episode ended as abruptly as it had begun. Dana reappeared on the landing, fully composed, that signature snarky grin on her ashen lips.

"That was gross," she joked. "Must have been something I ate."

Malia was not amused.

"So, is that how you gon' play this?" she yelled. "Cuz, if it is, I'm getting on the phone to Momma right now. Don't play with me. Not about this, D."

"I'm not playing," Dana replied, suddenly serious. "I know I messed up. But I know what I need to do. Last week, I heard about a new treatment center, a clinical trial for new trippers like me. If you're ready, I mean, if you definitely want to stop, they can get you moving in the right direction after only a three-day stay. Plus, it don't cost nothin'—just need to sign some papers saying they can use whatever they learn to help others."

The entire time she was talking, Dana busied herself in the kitchen, emptying the dishwasher, sweeping the already swept floor—anything to keep from making eye contact. Unlike most addicts, averting her eyes didn't mean she was lying; more often than not, it meant she was embarrassed.

Malia listened intently, both to Dana's words and her tone. Pushing away the feeling she was being deceived by wishful thinking, she decided to believe Dana. Anyway, what choice did she have?

"So, let's say I trust you and don't call in reinforcements," she said. "What happens now?"

Dana stopped what she was doing and turned to face her sister, suspicious of the fact that the master interrogator would let her off this easy.

"Well, this is the holiday week. You're off work, right? If you can take the boys, I'll head over to the clinic tonight, do my time, and then get the kids from you at Momma's when we all come over for Thanksgiving dinner. That'll even give me some time to catch up with Terran so we can talk for real."

By now, Malia was leaning against the back door, staring out the window. The sun was bright now, but she knew it was still bitterly cold outside. *Deception.* The word kept playing over and over in her mind.

Only God can make a freezing winter day look so sunny and warm. And only happy-go-lucky Dana can sprinkle stardust and moonbeams on such a catastrophic situation and make it feel all better.

"Trust and believe this, D," Malia warned. "If you're not at Momma's by two o'clock Thursday, you better start getting used to life without your kids."

At that moment, there was a loud bang, and then squeals emanated from behind the living room sofa.

"The boys are up," Dana announced. "Help me pack."

EIGHTEEN

Consequences

So Dana's shit is definitely raggedy, but hey, at least she sees it. What's that old saying? "The first step is admitting you have a problem."

Well, Terran, your turn.

♥

FOR A MOMENT, Terran had no idea where he was. His head was pounding, and every time he tried to open his eyes, red and yellow flashes of light forced them to slam shut again. His back hurt, no doubt because of how he had so awkwardly positioned his body on the narrow steel frame and stained, wire-punctured pad masquerading as a mattress. There were so many sounds, some uncomfortably close: snorts, coughs, and growls—human, Terran hoped. Other noises echoed in the distance: the incessant *beeping* of a two-way radio…phones ringing…an antique-sounding copy machine… What eventually coaxed Terran into full consciousness was the smell—a combination of liquor, sweat, urine, and feces, a stench so thick that, for a second, he considered the pros and cons of not breathing at all.

"Jackson, Terran C.," a baritone voice called. Out of nowhere, Amos Franklin, a large, red-faced Jackson County Detention Unit officer, appeared in the cell door. Though the marred gray-white bars were wide open, not one of the eight other occupants made a move. Unlike Terran, they knew the drill. Sure, the police had busted them all together last night at the crack house, but until the officer called your name, it was best to keep a low profile.

Terran rolled off the cot and raised his hand. "Here," he grunted.

His mind raced as he walked timidly towards the opening. Unlike most brothers he knew, the previous night was his first time in jail. Too embarrassed to call anyone, he had opted to stay in jail and figure out the bail thing in the morning.

Officer Franklin sensed Terran's hesitation.

"Hey, man, stop sweating," he said. "If you play your cards right, today could be your lucky day."

"Yeah, right," Terran scoffed, so eager to get out of there that he stubbed his toe on the back of the officer's thick rubber heel. "I can think of a lot of words for this situation. Lucky ain't one of them."

"Look, when you came in last night, eyes all glassy, ashamed and dejected, it didn't take a rocket scientist to see you aren't about this life," Franklin explained. "Lucky for you, Dr. G. was at the booking desk, answering a call from one of his 'finds.' He saw what we saw, and here we are."

Dr. G, also known as Alejandro Gonzalez, was head of the True Grit Center, a medical facility for innovative—some might argue *unorthodox*—addiction treatment methods. His newest program, Squash It, was an intense, in-patient experience designed exclusively for crack cocaine users in deep enough to recognize they had a problem but not so deep they no longer had anything to lose.

The program was simple. After an intrusive personal interview and background check, patients spent three days under lockdown, drying out cold turkey. For 20 hours a day, users existed in a closet-sized cubicle—a cell, really—surrounded by wall-sized images representing the casualties of their addiction. (The intense realness of this particular part of the treatment would take Terran's breath away: Dana at high school graduation, their half-eaten wedding cake, TJ with his new Hot Wheels trike, Terran's first day as shift supervisor.) Besides intense, small-group counseling, they paired each patient with a "mirror," a program graduate and recovering addict whose "how I got here" story was so strikingly similar to their own that you'd swear they'd scripted it. Participants got little sleep, which compelled them to verbalize every perverted, despondent, and self-deprecating thought that popped into their heads. The program admitted everyone on scholarship, and an anonymous ex-addict benefactor, supplemented by public funds, covered the expenses.

Despite its obvious benefits, Squash It was definitely not for everyone. You could enter the program only through a referral. And if, in the interviewer's opinion, you weren't unquestionably enthusiastic about engaging in real talk, ADMISSION DENIED. Not surprisingly, the dropout rate was high, but when the program was successful, recidivism rates were significantly lower than any other treatment center in the state.

Before Terran could form a coherent question, Officer Franklin nudged him through a narrow doorway, up five short stairs, down an unexpectedly bright hallway, and into a gigantic conference room with floor-to-ceiling windows overlooking an elementary school playground.

"We don't lock this door," Franklin warned. "If you know what's good for you, you won't even think about leaving."

Uncertain what to do, Terran pressed his face against the ice-cold windowpane and squinted toward the sunlight. Taking quick breaths to calm himself, he tried to arrange the previous night's memories into a narrative that made some kind of sense.

NINETEEN

Busted

B Y NOW, TERRAN KNEW THE DRILL.

When you reach the end of the block, turn the corner and slow down to no more than 10 miles per hour. Maintain that speed until you reach the dead oak tree. Turn off the headlights, ease forward, parallel to the garage door, flash your lights, and wait. A sentry will step out and tap your passenger-side window. At that time of night, the man on duty was probably J.C., a tall chocolate-brown brother who played high school basketball with Terran back in the day.

"Same ol' same ol', two dimes, $20?" J.C. asked.

"Nah, man," Terran responded. "I need a little more today. Ask Landon if I can get a teenager for $40. I'm a good customer."

J.C. cracked the house's back door open just enough for a stream of light to spill out. He tilted his head, never taking his eyes off Terran. Whispers ensued, followed by what sounded like someone ripping gift wrap.

"$45," J.C. responded definitively.

Transaction made, Terran eased the car forward through the alley. As he turned onto 29th Street and flicked on his headlights, all hell broke loose. Suddenly the streets next to the alley and in front of the crack house were awash with counterfeit illumination.

"Show me your hands!" a voice yelled.

A bald black police officer appeared from out of nowhere. Terran put the car in park, unfastened his seatbelt, and placed both hands as far out of the driver-side window as humanly possible. Seconds later, his door flew open, and what felt like a thousand hands began push-pulling him from his seat. Startled by the noise, his initial instinct was to fight back.

"Down!" a pistol-wielding female officer with a blonde ponytail demanded as her partner slammed Terran's face into the gravel.

Now voices echoed from all sides, each shouting their own version of the same command. With his face in the dirt and his arms bent back awkwardly as the small but powerful blonde attached zip ties to his wrists, all Terran could see were feet—thick black boots surrounding his car and two other pairs halfway down the block...scruffy tennis shoes and pastel-pink toenails in blinged-out sandals running from the direction of the crack house, with more of those boots in hot pursuit.

Given how Terran had been living, getting caught up in a drug bust should have come as no surprise. He watched the TV show *Cops*. But foolishly, he had convinced himself that the chances of it happening to him were slim. He was careful. He usually scored in the open, on street corners or bus stops—and only from people he knew. Since the awful scene Dana had walked in on, he had vowed to stay away from drug houses. He'd driven by the bus stop earlier that night, but no one had been out. *Landon's place would be safe*, he had told himself. Hell, the dude had lookouts with pagers covering a four-block radius.

Somebody missed something, and now I'm fucked, Terran lamented as he joined Landon, J.C., and twelve other misfortunates in the back of the white police van. He had all but accepted the fact that he and Dana were over, but until tonight, he'd still had his kids and his job to cling to.

It's *all gone now,* he thought, tears forming in his tightly closed eyes.

Fortunately for him, God had other plans.

TWENTY

Big Boy Pants

ACCORDING TO DR. GONZALES, the fact that Terran had breezed through the Squash It program's admittance process was a very good sign. Terran wasn't as sure, that is until he met the mirror assigned to his case. Tawana St. John was tall for a woman, nearly six feet, with cocoa-colored skin, striking green eyes, and voluptuous curves. Forget the polite platitudes: this woman was *hot*. As was customary, their first encounter took place at The Spot, an indoor courtyard located at the intersection of the patient cubicles beneath a huge skylight. Thanks to the "open kimono" clause in the Squash It contract, the two were already intimately acquainted. Though Squash It gives its investigators only 24 hours to compile intake profiles, the final mirror-to-mirror info-packets were *dense*: medical records, counselors' notes, and even audio tapes of private conversations between patient, psychiatrist, family, and friends.

"The content is raw," Dr. G. had warned. "But take the time, work through it, and in a few hours, you'll have everything you need to know to make a real difference in the life of your partner."

Not everything, Terran mused, trying not to stare.

The sessions began just after lunch on day two. Outside, the air was brisk, and the sun was beaming. Inside, the mood was anything but bright. Dr. G. and six other patients lounged silently on bright orange beanbags. In the center of the circle, Terran and Tawana sat face to face, straddling a worn wooden bench. The two had been at each other's throats for nearly an hour, having careened right through the typical pleasantries of first-time meetings to bare their souls.

"Whatever, Terran. You can't bullshit a bullshitter," Tawana interrupted, her formal Canadian accent masking intense emotions. "I used to blame everyone else, too. First it was my mother, who *let me* move from Toronto to attend Clark Atlanta University on a music scholarship. Then there was Nick, my ex-husband, who *got me* pregnant and *tricked* me into putting my career on hold so we could move to Kansas City to expand his law practice," Tawana huffed sarcastically, rubbing her sweaty palms on her tight denim skirt.

"For five years, I played the role: doting mother to twin girls, dutiful stay-at-home wife. Perfect, right up until my Nicky starts trading prostitute pussy for legal services. And how did I find out? The bastard gave me AIDs."

Terran blinked nervously and lifted his face toward the skylight. No one else moved.

"That's fucked up, Tawana," he said. "But at least you don't have to endure some lame-ass job to feed your kids. If I had your coin, I wouldn't give a shit."

Tawana closed her eyes and tried to visualize the right response, a technique she had just learned in-program.

"At the risk of sounding sexist, why do men always attribute their fuck-ups to money?" she said. "Hey, Dr. G. Let's explore *that.*"

With that, Tawana opened the floodgates, recounting how her unlimited bank account had allowed her to live in denial for months, burning up thousands of dollars in an underground private club, smoking weed, and watching but not taking part in the nightly passing of the pipes. The night Nick confessed (yeah, he did it, but divorce was out of the question—bad for business), Tawana made a mad dash to the club, counted out five crisp one-hundred-dollar bills to the drug dealer masquerading as a bartender, and went on a three-day bender with the purest cocaine in the city.

At first, feeding her addiction was easy. His antics exposed, Nick began staying away from home for weeks at a time. He kept tabs on the girls through neighbors and almost-daily phone calls—*everything's fine, Daddy,* Tawana coached them to say. But as long as

Tawana didn't put his business in the streets, Nick paid little attention to the bank balance. The party ended abruptly when, six months into the chaos, a neighbor discovered Tawana passed out on the bathroom floor as thick black smoke billowed out her kitchen window; the six-year-old twins had nearly burned down the house trying to make grilled cheese sandwiches.

The neighbor called the school. The school called the police. Once the media got wind of the situation, all the money in the world couldn't contain the story. The couple split immediately; Nick had a reputation to protect. Her husband agreed to pay alimony but demanded sole custody of the girls. In exchange, the prosecutor (one of Nick's former colleagues) would drop the drug abuse and child endangerment charges and help Tawana secure an interview with Squash It.

"Pressure, whether emotional, financial, or otherwise, can trigger crazy impulses," Tawana explained. "But what you do with those impulses is your responsibility. *Yours*. No one else's."

"So I should blame life," Terran sniped. "Not my manic boss. Not my ball-buster wife. Not my needy family."

"That's how *I* sleep at night," Tawana replied. "Besides, blame goes both ways. The bastard who pushed me over the edge is also the angel who probably saved my life."

TWENTY ONE

Eyes Wide Open

"There are none so blind as those who will not see."

— John Heywood, 1546

THE WHIZ-BANG OF THE FURNACE kicking in jolted Terran awake. It was the Monday before Thanksgiving, only four days since that fateful morning at the police station, and he was home alone. Given the profound changes that had occurred in his life, it felt as if years had passed. Because the police had picked him up the Wednesday before his planned two-week vacation, he had completed his three days on-site completely off the grid, his boss and his wife none the wiser. As he sat up to get his bearings, waves of anxiety washed over him. *Panic attack.* Terran slammed his eyes shut, struggling to quiet his mind. His palms began to sweat, his neck tensed, and his chest hurt, just like last week in jail. And yesterday, with Dana.

After the brief but emotional Squash It graduation ceremony, Terran had rushed right home, full of hope. As he pulled into the driveway that bright Sunday morning, he couldn't help but smile at how pleasantly ordinary the house appeared. *I need to cut the grass,* he noted, shoving his key into the finicky lock. As soon as the foyer filled with light, reality hit him like a punch in the gut: the sweet little cottage he and Dana had been so proud of was no more. Ignoring for the moment the lifeless lump lying half-on, half-off the sofa, Terran dropped his bag at the foot of the stairs and leaned against the banister to take in his surroundings. It's not that it was unkempt, he observed. The house appeared *unloved.* Terran was 99 percent positive he'd only been away two weeks. How in God's name could this have happened so fast?

Since the curtains were still drawn, the view through the living room to the kitchen was dim, but not so dark as to mask the sad scene. Except for the large stack of unopened mail on the coffee table and the crusted-over takeout boxes on the kitchen counter, both rooms were relatively neat. The rug looked vacuumed, and there were no clothes on the floor or dishes in the sink. *A place for everything and everything in its place,* Dana used to insist. Still, the house was missing any signs of life: no Hot Wheels cars or broken crayons strewn haphazardly about, no half-eaten sweet treats in the sugar-coated cake carrier on the counter, and no spicy aromas from simmering pots on the stove. The air was stale, as if someone had died here long ago. His throat suddenly dry, Terran made his way to the refrigerator in search of a beer. *It's five o'clock somewhere,* he reasoned. Except for the familiar, red-stained plastic Kool-Aid pitcher and some unrecognizable leftovers wrapped in aluminum foil, the fridge was empty.

While the overall atmosphere was disturbing, for Terran, the scene beneath the living room windows was downright horrifying. His once-curvaceous wife's nearly nude, emaciated frame was partially concealed under a thin plaid blanket. Her dry, matted hair peeked out from one end of the sofa; a freshly scarred foot caked with dirt and blood dangled from the other. As if he needed further confirmation, on the floor, spilling out of Dana's purse, was the missing crack pipe.

Terran sat down on the stairs and rubbed his eyes. Though she'd yet to move a muscle, he could tell she was awake. Psychic for each other—he and Dana had always been like that.

Boy, you've got a sixth sense about that girl, his mother would say.

"Are the boys with Malia?" he asked in a voice so calm he surprised even himself. "We gotta talk."

TWENTY TWO

Confessions Of A Crack Daddy

S TRANGE HOW YOU KNOW THINGS before you even *know* you
know.

That Sunday, even in her hungover state, Dana sensed
something was different about her husband as soon as he entered
the front door. Maybe it was the sound of Terran's footsteps as he
inspected their house—slow, cautious, not like someone who lived
there. In her mind's eye, she could see him on the stairs, knees
against the railing, absentmindedly scratching the nape of his neck
as he always did when he had something important to say.

Oh, well, Dana thought. *We might as well get this over with.*

"I'm picking the boys up on Thursday," she said, her head still
covered. "Thanksgiving at Momma's."

"Good, good," Terran replied.

The way he said it, almost as though he were talking to himself, made Dana sit up and take notice, allowing the blanket to fall to the floor. It had been months since Terran had seen her in her underwear. True to form, he didn't even pretend to hide his shock.

"Jesus, D," he gasped. "Skin *and* bones."

"Whatever, Terran. You're no Incredible Hulk yourself," Dana replied. "We both know what's up, but I'm handling it. You said you wanted to talk, so talk."

And talk, he did. As Dana gazed out the now-open curtains, Terran paced back and forth, recounting the events of the past week as if he were performing a play: the police raid on Landon's house, his first-ever night in jail, Dr. G, the Squash It program, and the unbelievably familiar stories of the other patients in his "quad."

"You're so far gone you didn't even realize I took our wedding photos and baby albums," he said with a sigh.

Though Dana was only half-listening, she suddenly realized something. For the first time in months, she and Terran were having a conversation. Sure, he was doing most of the talking, but the fact that there was no yelling, profanity, or finger-pointing was noteworthy—and there was something else. Whenever the stories turned emotional—as Terran's eyes sparkled and his voice cracked—one name emerged: Tawana.

There was the first Squash It breakfast, when he'd forced his quad mates to listen to him whine about his job and the unfair way they doled out promotions. It was Tawana who had called bullshit.

"Did you ever think maybe your *attitude* is limiting your *altitude?*" she had inserted.

Or, in the middle of the night, when he'd tried to run, sweating through withdrawals and bawling his eyes out in front of the life-sized cutouts of TJ and Tyler, it had been Tawana who'd comforted him.

Dana was sensing a pattern, but nothing could have prepared her for what Terran would announce next.

"Excuse me?" she said, astounded. "You're moving in with some crackhead AIDs patient you met four days ago?"

"Look, I know how fucked up this is," Terran admitted. "But I'm a hundred percent positive this is what I need right now to maintain my sobriety. We're no longer good together—you know that as well as I do—and anyway, lately the boys have been with Malia more than with us."

"And about *your* situation," Terran continued, "if you say you're handling it, I'll believe you. I'll keep paying the bills for now—but that won't last forever."

Terran made his way to the couch and got down on one knee, determined to make eye contact. As he reached for her, Dana recoiled, positioning herself as far away from this stranger as possible without leaving her seat.

Startled by the force of Dana's rejection, Terran sat back.

"I'm just gonna grab a few things from upstairs," he said. "I'll check back with y'all after the holidays. We can talk more then, okay?"

"Wow," Dana said. "Just...wow."

As Terran's words filled the space between them, the now officially estranged husband and wife sat quietly for several minutes.

"I heard about that program," Dana reflected. "Me and Tina 'been trying everything to get a referral. She convinced me it was the miracle you and I needed to fix our family."

Suddenly furious, Dana bolted from the sofa, nearly trampling her husband.

"What a crock!" she shouted. "Some fix! Well, you know what? Fuck Squash It! Fuck your sobriety. And fuck you, Terran Jackson. I'm done."

And thus began the last week of Dana Lawton Jackson's time on earth.

TWENTY THREE

Get Out

Somebody once said harboring anger is like drinking poison and expecting the other person to die. Well, Dana, cheers!

♥

STUCK. V. Incapable of moving forward, unable to escape.

In therapy, the term refers to an emotional state. For addicts, being stuck means being trapped on a bender, typically at the drug house, physically unable to put down the pipe, bong, or syringe for hours, sometimes days. Relatively speaking, Dana was still a novice user, but she'd seen this movie before. And no matter who the actors are, how honorable their intentions, or how strong their resolve in other aspects of their lives, once someone is "in the trap," the episode always ends the same. Still, somehow, Dana had convinced herself that this time would be different. It didn't take much to pretend, just a healthy dose of denial and some creative self-talk—something like this:

I'm Jonesing, but I don't have much time. I could take the stuff home, but the kids are there. Maybe cook in the car again? Ugh, that's dangerous.

By the time you get to the spot, you're anxious, not thinking. You jump through the hoops, say the secret password, and *boom*, you're inside. Money and merchandise change hands, and finally you caress that magic rock between thumb and forefinger. Your heart races and it occurs to you: *Why not stay here? It's quiet. They have lookouts. I can be in and out in 15 minutes, 30 tops.* Decision made, you step over nondescript bodies passed out on the floor and maneuver your way to the farthest corner of the room. The place is dreary, smelly, but also serene...except for the occasional tussle between patrons not happy with a slow-to-pass-it pipe hog. For a moment, you feel invisible, safe. But that anonymity fades as soon as you fire up.

Except for the cadre of strangers watching your every move, for the first hit or two, you have the pipe all to yourself. Soon beads of sweat dot your upper lip as you concede the fact that it's time to pass it. Share or get shanked—those are the house rules. You pass right and look left—thankfully, you're not the only one financing this party. In this communal space, there's something for everyone: crackheads and freebasers swap paraphernalia with sniffers, needle shooters, and marijuana smokers. The rituals are, in a word, hypnotic. Between hits, those who still have something to live for see flashes of their responsibilities outside: the car wash, picking up kids from daycare, fending off familiar "late again?" scowls at work. In the dark recesses of your brain you hear screaming: *get out, go home, anywhere but here.* Your body doesn't listen. "I gotta go," you announce for the umpteenth time, though, deep down, you know you're not going anywhere. Minutes turn into hours, and hours into days. At this point, your ass might as well be super-glued to the floor.

Dana lay motionless on a bare mattress in one of MJ the Dope Man's side rooms, desperate to hang on to her buzz. Too late—the post-high melancholy was already beginning to set in. It was after 10:00 p.m., almost nine hours since her husband's big announcement. If there had been any doubt about the state of their relationship before, all questions had been answered when her profanity-laden tongue-lashing elicited no response. The image was seared into her brain: Terran just sitting there, exhausted, a mix of pity and pain in his eyes. *Enough!* Dana had decided. *Time to go.*

Before her husband could make his way back downstairs, she had hastily wrapped her shoes, clothes, and purse in the blanket and run, barefoot and freezing, the 13 blocks across town to where she now lay. She could have hit up Landon's place around the corner, but that was Terran's spot. After that fateful day when she first discovered her husband's secret, Dana had vowed to never set foot in that place again.

From the crack house office (also known as the kitchen), Dana could hear MJ and his cousin Tyrone clinking beer bottles and chattering incessantly. The men were hunched over a small Formica-top table covered with cash and merchandise as Monte the Mortician, one of their best customers, looked on hungrily from a folding chair in the hallway.

"Hey, Monte, I think your passenger is about to rise up and call a cab," Tyrone announced sarcastically.

Lamont "Monte" Jacobs drove the pick-up van for the Leon B. Jacobs Funeral Home, the oldest black-owned family business in the city. His "passenger" was an 86-year-old corpse retrieved the previous evening from the Sunset Grove Senior Care Center. Though both the authorities and his uncle/employer insisted cadavers take no detours on the way to the morgue, it was a holiday week, and according to the cute nurse at the center, Dead Guy had no family.

He won't care if I stop in for a quick hit, Monte had reasoned. That had been 20 hours ago. *Stuck.*

MJ was pretty sure Monte's Uncle Jake wouldn't call the police (too much publicity), but it was only a matter of time before he came looking for his property.

"Seriously, man," he demanded, "you need to bounce."

Dana half-watched as Monte peeled himself off the dusty brown seat cushion, picked up his jacket, and sauntered closer than necessary to the office table on his way to the door. Suddenly two loud gunshots pierced the silence. Dana instinctively rolled off the mattress and dove behind the bed, landing squarely atop April and Sanaa, two emaciated teenagers also trying to avoid the line of fire.

"I'm sorry, man. Please don't kill me!" Monte begged.

Teeth clenched, MJ shoved the hot-barreled Colt .45 into the would-be thief's crusty, dry mouth and snatched six stolen rocks from Monte's sweaty hand. As he was considering whether or not to pull the trigger, Omani, MJ's four-year-old daughter, wandered into the kitchen.

"Daddy, I'm scared," she cried. Immediately, MJ released Lamont and shielded the gun behind his back.

"It's ok, baby. I'm sorry we talkin' too loud. Go on back to bed," MJ coaxed.

The distraction gave Monte just enough time to make a mad dash for the door. He exited the alley slower than usual, stunned that none of the heavily armed sentries tried to stop him.

Thank you, God, Monte prayed, knowing a return to this establishment would cost him his life.

Inside, it was business as usual. Tyrone and MJ were at the table, and Sanaa and April had crawled back to their previous spots on the burn room floor. Once again, Dana was on the mattress, lying on her back, her forearms covering her eyes.

"Stealing from MJ? That man must have a death wish," Sanaa said.

"He always been *crazy* like that," April drawled in her Lower Alabama accent.

"Shit," Dana replied. "Anything, even death, has to be better than this."

The girls chuckled at what they thought to be the weird, sometimes dark sarcasm they'd come to expect from "the funny girl with the light eyes."

Dana wasn't laughing.

TWENTY FOUR

Baller

DANA.

L enita rolled out of bed and scooped up the ringing phone in a single motion. She was groggy but not surprised. No, her phone didn't have caller ID, but who else could it be? BC— "before crack"—a midnight call would disrupt the entire Marcus household. First there was Gavin, Lenita's husband and a decorated captain in the Kansas City Police Department. This guy *lived* on RED ALERT.

"What's wrong, is your momma ok?" he would ask, lights on, shoes in hand. "I can be there in 12 minutes."

Next came the patter of bare feet on hardwood, followed by anxious tapping on the bedroom door.

"I'm going with Daddy," Alex would proclaim.

Before, chaos, but now, at least for Lenita's family, Dana's antics had become so commonplace that these late-night calls barely registered. Lenita tip-toed into the hallway and closed the door. Silence from her son's room, and Gavin's rhythmic snores never missed a beat. While her family pretty much ignored the interruptions, Lenita thanked God for these calls. Thanks to Malia, everyone but Momma D knew all about Dana's and Terran's drug problems. Not surprisingly, the pair had started to make themselves scarce, even skipping the last few Sunday dinners. Lenita had been calling her sister for weeks, but to no avail. Last Saturday, she had discovered the phone had been disconnected. She'd even tried dropping by unexpectedly, but Dana never seemed to be home. In the end, all Lenita could do was pray that her troubled sister would reach out to her.

"Hey, what'chu doing?" Dana asked, too cheerful for the hour.

"Uh, sleeping," Lenita barked. "Are you okay?"

"Yeah, I'm good," Dana responded trying to sound upbeat, though her voice was shaking. "But something happened, and I want to make sure somebody knows where I am."

This can't be good, Lenita thought with a sigh, and she settled in at the top of the stairs.

For the next hour, Dana unloaded about Terran getting busted, his recovery, and his decision to leave his family for his new crackhead girlfriend—the reason she had decided not to pursue the Squash It program she had been so excited about days earlier.

Dana even opened up about the shooting at the crack house and how she definitely was terrified, but also intrigued.

"This might sound crazy," she confessed, "but I'm starting to wonder why everybody's so scared of dying. To me, heaven's sounding pretty awesome right about now."

This revelation felt like pinpricks to Lenita's heart. How could such a strong, positive, happy-go-lucky person end up in such a hopeless predicament?

Lenita buried her emotions as she always did during these encounters, speaking only to flesh out details that might prove important later. She knew Malia had already freaked out and issued Dana an ultimatum: Be at Thanksgiving dinner by 2:00 p.m., or we'll bring in the big guns—Momma, the police, and Family Services. By offering a sympathetic ear, Lenita hoped to alleviate any fears her sister might have about facing the family. Maybe if Dana believed she had at least one non-judgmental ally, she would keep her promise. On the other hand, playing "good cop" to Malia's "bad cop" could also backfire.

"It's quiet where you are now," Lenita said. "Are you at MJ's?"

The reference to past visits to the crack house helped Dana snap back into the present.

"Naw, girl, that's why I called you," Dana squealed. "I'm at Bobby Ames's condo!"

I must be hearing things, Lenita thought. Throughout their conversation, she'd been watching two squirrels enjoying an early breakfast in the neighbor's oak tree, anticipating the sunrise. Soon the streetlights would go out, and the city would come alive.

Standing up to stretch, she chuckled. "I *know* I'm tripping. For a minute, I thought you said Bobby Ames, as in the baseball player."

"That's exactly what I said," Dana confirmed. "Bobby Ray Ames, second basemen, 1990 World Series superstar. He came in the crack house a few hours ago, flashing cash and ready to party. So far, he's been cool, no drama. But a few minutes ago, Bobby and two of his friends went to get more rocks, or so they said. Thing is, he left me and Crystal, this teenage stripper, locked in. If we try to leave, alarms go off, cops show up."

For Lenita, the assertion that a famous athlete like Ames would be so bold (or stupid) as to show his face at a crack house was too bizarre to accept at face value. But apparently, when he strolled into MJ's kitchen, high-fiving the crew as if he were attending an autograph session, Dana had been the only person surprised. According to Sanaa and April, Ames was a frequent customer who liked to share.

"We got with him lots of times," they'd told Dana. "He's always nice, especially to new girls. Act right, and he'll give you whatever you want."

Party on, Dana had decided. To her delight, the pseudo-celebrity had noticed her immediately. Even in her emaciated state, *this* new girl looked good. After some flirty banter about which major league team had the hottest players, Dana and Crystal, a big-breasted 18-year-old runaway, were invited to take a ride in the famous royal-blue Escalade.

"Dana, you know this is crazy, right?" Lenita yelled, judgmental as hell. "What if he comes back with five other guys who aren't so nice? What's the address?"

"I don't know," Dana answered. "We came in through a parking garage. It's still kinda dark outside, but I can see apartment buildings and houses out the window, so I know we're not downtown. Bobby's place is on the top floor. Maybe South Kansas City? Or Leawood.

"That's *so* not helpful," Lenita said. "Did you see any street signs?"

Suddenly Dana's voice dropped to a whisper, and there was a rustling in the background.

"Nita, somebody's coming! Go back to bed. I'll call you tonight."

Dial tone. Lenita stared at the receiver for several minutes and then rubbed her weary eyes. *Might as well make the coffee,* she conceded. There would be no more sleeping today.

TWENTY FIVE

Five's A Crowd

AFTER HANGING UP ON HER SISTER, Dana maneuvered around the huge marble island in the baseball legend's massive kitchen and planted herself cross-legged on the butter-soft leather sofa where Crystal lay sleeping. The voices she'd heard earlier were now right outside the condo door.

Lenita was right. More rock wasn't the only thing her host had picked up on his second drug run of the evening. The party was definitely larger—three or four more guys by her estimation. And this group was *loud*. Panicked, Dana gave Crystal a series of hard nudges until the girl's bloodshot eyes appeared to hold some semblance of focus.

"Hear that? This shit's about to get real."

"Whatever," Crystal said with a shrug, "as long as they scored."

As the door opened, the room fell silent. Bobby entered first, all smiles, followed by Skinny Boy Jake, a well-known user Dana had met weeks ago at MJ's, and three large, tattooed, stone-faced thugs in matching leather vests. Determined to take control of the situation, Dana sauntered over to Bobby, extended her hand, and willed her face to convey something akin to lust.

"You and me?" she asked seductively, remembering what Sanaa had said about her host's preference for the new girl.

In a definitive gesture of acceptance, Bobby pulled Dana close and retrieved five small bags from the breast pocket of his fox fur coat. He handed two to Dana and placed the rest on the teak coffee table. He tossed his coat to the floor, tipped his imaginary cap, and led his date toward the bedroom. As the door closed behind them, Dana watched Jake pull a well-worn crack pipe from his pocket and join Crystal on the sofa. The rest of the crew positioned themselves on the floor between the table legs and Crystal's bare feet. As the tallest of the three prepared a second pipe, the other two conspired to coax the distracted girl out of her skin-tight jeans.

It felt as if only moments had passed, but it was after 6:00 a.m., hours later, when Dana, Bobby, and the rest of the crew began to crash. Of course, no one was sleepy, and eating was out of the question. While Bobby was in the bathroom throwing up for the second time, Dana returned to the living room to join Crystal. Her now-topless   partner-in-crime   appeared   shell-shocked, absentmindedly picking at old scabs as the other guys stared into space. Everyone knew what the other was thinking.

"We'll make one more run," Bobby announced, his mood oddly euphoric as he wiped his mouth with the back of his hand.

Determined to end this night with a modicum of dignity, Dana grabbed her shoes and bolted for the door.

"Hold up. Y'all can't go," Bobby protested. "Not enough room in the truck."

"Come on, baby, we can sit on laps," Dana cooed. "Besides, when y'all were gone, I think I heard somebody in the hallway whispering and slamming doors."

With that revelation, happiness turned into paranoia. Nosy neighbors, Bobby did *not* need.

"Load up. We all gettin' out of here right now," he agreed.

Safe at Home

The Willie Mays Aikens Story

ALTHOUGH *THE SIN-SICK SOUL* IS A WORK OF FICTION, the character of the cocaine-addicted athlete was inspired by a real person, former Kansas City Royals first baseman Willie Mays Aikens, who opened up about his challenges with drug abuse in a 2012 biography by sportswriter Gregory Jordan.

Safe at Home[3] uses vivid imagery and heartfelt prose to chronicle Aikens's rise from the dusty cotton fields of Seneca, South Carolina, to become the first player in major league history with two multi-home run games in the World Series. According to former teammate and hall-of-fame third baseman George Brett, on the field, Aikens was a force to be reckoned with.

"He was a threat every time he got a bat in his hand," Brett said in a 2010 interview with Amy K. Nelson, senior correspondent for sports blog network SB Nation.

"He wasn't freaked out, he didn't panic with two strikes; he didn't even freak out when a tough left-hander was on the mound."

What Brett and other teammates likely did not know: Aikens's blasé, unflappable approach to the game was a side effect of his constant drug use.

"Every day, every game of the [1980] series, I snorted cocaine," Aikens told Nelson. "It had become part of my life."

Ironically, it was this unparalleled success that fueled Aikens's belief that everything was under control—his drug use was not a problem.

"I hit two home runs in the first game of the World Series," he recalled. "I mean, I had a tremendous second half in 1980. We had just whipped the New York Yankees three games to zero. I had just driven in the winning run in the last game of the playoffs against the Yankees, against Ron Guidry, who had dominated me the whole year. At that time, there wasn't anything in my life to say, 'Willie, you shouldn't be doing this.'"

Three short years later, Aikens and three of his teammates, Willie Wilson, Vida Blue, and Jerry Martin, became the first active players in Major League Baseball history to go to jail. In 1983, Aikens was convicted of misdemeanor cocaine possession. He copped a plea and served only 81 days of a one-year jail sentence.

But as far as Major League Baseball was concerned, the sentence was life—Aikens's U.S. baseball career was over.

By the early 1990s, Aikens was back in Kansas City, living like a hermit. He had spent the past 10 years playing baseball in Mexico, smoking crack cocaine, and entertaining prostitutes.

"I always wanted a new girl," he recalled. That preference for "new meat" made Aikens a prime target for an FBI sting, during which he purchased more than 50 grams of crack from an undercover female agent. Aikens would soon discover how much the legal system had changed since his first conviction. New laws set penalties for possession and distribution of crack as much as 15 times higher than punishment for powdered cocaine. Convinced the laws were discriminatory (at the time, the crack epidemic disproportionately impacted poor, African-American communities), Aikens fought the charges. He lost the case and was sentenced to 20 years and eight months in prison.

Mandatory sentencing guidelines for possession and distribution of crack cocaine were eventually deemed cruel and unusual, and Aikens was released after 14 years. In a life-altering gesture, Brett introduced Aikens, who spoke fluent Spanish, to Royals general manager Dayton Moore. Assured the once-unstoppable talent was now clean and sober, Moore hired Aikens as a hitting instructor and consultant for South American recruits.

Kudos to Aikens for prevailing against the odds. If only not-so-famous crackheads could be so fortunate.

TWENTY SIX

Snatch And Dash

THE AIR IN BOBBY'S TOO-CROWDED SUV was thick with anticipation. Seven adults were literally sitting on top of each other, no one speaking, each tormented by after-high angst. The orange hint of sunrise was already visible when they reached the alley behind MJ's, but the "all clear" porch lights were still on. To be safe, Bobby had called ahead. Too many same-day visits made MJ nervous—nothing more dangerous than a junkie who has run out of money. This time, the spotters directed the motley crew to park on the street and walk the half-block to the crack house door. Seeing no armed doorman, Bobby tapped three times before turning the knob. MJ was in his usual spot at the kitchen table, shirtless and shoeless, the .45 resting on his lap.

"Long night?" MJ teased as Bobby initiated a handshake that shrouded three crisp one-hundred-dollar bills. "It's cool, though. I'm all for keeping the party going."

Like hungry school children in the cafeteria line, Dana, Crystal, and the others shuffled single file as one rock each was passed from MJ to Bobby to their shaky hands. During the ride over, everyone had already agreed that the party that night would end at MJ's—things were getting too hot at the condo. Dana was the first to make a move toward the burn room, determined to get as far away as possible from anyone who had borne witness to the things she'd done that night. She settled on an old sofa cushion on the floor beside the fireplace, took the crack pipe from her pocket, and faced the wall. Though every part of her was screaming for a fix, for a moment, she paused. With her back to the party crowd, she envisioned the bevy of freshly lit rocks sparkling like yellow-orange gems. Pipes crackled and hissed, and the thick black smoke made her eyes water.

Just as she was about to ignite her own flame, a sudden outbreak of high-pitched laughter captured her attention. Two rooms away, on the fenced-in porch reserved for "big ballers," MJ and Bobby were holding court, sipping expensive Scotch whiskey and lounging on black leather recliners.

"That bitch Dana is a freak," Bobby mused. "Last night, I turned her every which way but loose. Now she's acting like she's in love."

"Yeah, I know. She's wild," MJ replied. "She looks like the girl next door, but for a 15-minute high, she'll fuck you like a seasoned hoe. A crackhead ain't shit."

The exchange itself did not surprise Dana. In "the life," users often face criticism for doing things they're not proud of. What infuriated her was the superiority these two assholes were trying to portray: they believed they were better than her. Dana had never been a sexual prude, but she'd always demanded respect. Hell, just that night, she'd manipulated her way out of a gang rape. The way she saw it, she'd hooked up with a cute, rich celebrity—*her* choice. The only reason she'd poured on the clingy "in love" act afterward was to keep the money flowing. She was *not* a victim.

Now triggered, Dana extinguished the lighter and began banging her forehead against the brick wall. Who was she kidding? Trading sexual favors for rocks? That's how weak-minded, powerless prostitutes behaved. MJ was right. *A crackhead ain't shit.*

It felt like a lifetime ago that Dana had lobbed this same insult at her husband, Terran. *Look at you now,* she thought. *Worthless.* Dana shook her head, reignited the lighter, and sucked in two long drags. As her lungs filled for the third time, shame morphed into anger, and anger gave way to full-on rage.

Why am I allowing these idiots to make the rules? Who died and left them in charge?

Dana pressed her soot-singed fingers to her temples and rose to her feet. Trying not to attract attention, she wrapped the still-warm pipe in her wool scarf, shoved it in her pocket, and strolled toward the back hallway. Anthony, a house spotter who had been trying to get her into bed for weeks, was lying face up on the cold tile floor.

"What's up?" he mumbled.

"I gotta pee," Dana teased, brushing her index finger across his muscular thigh.

Once inside the bathroom, Dana pre-flushed the toilet and closed the door. After waiting a few minutes to establish her whereabouts, she snuck out an adjacent door that led through the kitchen to a side exit. On the table, most likely because Bobby's "big money" crew were the only users on the premises, MJ had left a smorgasbord of cash, rocks, and weed unattended.

"Fuck you, MJ," Dana growled, stuffing the entire haul into her underwear. *Power restored.*

What Dana didn't know was that MJ's side exit was secured by lock and key. What's more, outside the kitchen exit, the early crew had already arrived. Nervous but not afraid, she decided her best chance of escape was to retrace her steps. Three minutes later, she was climbing out the bathroom window, shoes in hand, her fate sealed. When MJ realized both his stash and one of his houseguests had gone missing, it would be "game over."

As she meandered through frozen backyards toward Momma D's house, the frigid air burning her chest, something occurred to Dana. Truth be told, she couldn't care less what MJ might do to her, but what if someone was following her? What if they came after her mother?

This wasn't the first time Dana had ended the evening sweating through her underwear, running for her life. Most often, focusing on the night sky calmed her, but not tonight. Thanksgiving was less than two days away. All hell would break loose if she didn't show up for dinner, but she couldn't think about that now. She needed a place to think without endangering her family.

Ninety-nine percent sure she was now in the clear, Dana slowed to a jog and then ducked into the always-open entryway door of an abandoned apartment building that, thanks to local churchgoers, housed the best makeshift homeless shelter in the city. Inside, Dana fell face down on the dirty tile floor.

"Lord, give me rest," she prayed aloud, not sure He was listening.

TWENTY SEVEN

Jesus 9-1-1

A BRILLIANT PHILOSOPHER—Lisa from *The Simpsons*—once called prayer "the last refuge of a scoundrel." That makes perfect, especially if you grew up in the hood.

Prayer is why the Baptist preacher caught with his hand in the till is so quick to preach forgiveness. It's also why your shady Cousin June Bug has no use for God until he goes to prison. Or why drug dealers show up in court clutching in Grandma's Bible.

And 9-1-1 religion is why, at 9:00 p.m. the night before Thanksgiving, Dana found herself crouching in the foyer of a makeshift homeless shelter, staring at the ornate steeple atop the church across the street. But unlike other sometimes Christians, Dana *knew* God. In fact, she and her Lord and Savior had been on a first-name basis since elementary school. What's more, Dana's faith was self-motivated. Sure, the spirit of God had always been present in her mother's home. Old-school gospel was the undisputed soundtrack of Sunday morning breakfast. And Dana couldn't recall a significant conversation with Momma D that didn't include a "Hallelujah," "Thank you, Jesus," or "God don't like ugly," depending on the situation. But unlike other families in the neighborhood for whom God's house was the place to be, the Lawtons weren't "church people"—no Sunday morning worship, no Wednesday night Bible study, and definitely no mandatory summers at vacation bible school. Working two, sometimes three jobs, it was all Momma D could handle to get her ten kids to do their homework and finish their chores each day without burning down the house. While Dana had heard about God at home, she found Jesus for herself in a 64-count box of Crayola crayons. And a learned preacher hadn't motivated her to embrace the Scriptures. Dana's spiritual eyes were first opened by a precocious fourth-grader with a broken leg.

Before the accident, nine-year-old Micah Sampson had already been dubbed a weird kid simply because he was so damn happy.

"Don't you *just* love homework?" he'd tease his annoyed classmates at Anna May Richardson Elementary School.

When rain meant no outside recess, Ms. Martin, his bifocal-wearing, slow-talking teacher, was happy to look the other way as he took over the class, making up stories and organizing lavish performances that kept the other students in stitches. It's no wonder Micah and Dana were drawn to each other. They lived at opposite ends of the same block and were being raised by especially fertile single mothers—Micah's mom had four girls and three other boys. Both also suffered from youngest child syndrome: attention junkies alternatively tortured and ignored by their older siblings.

On that sultry August afternoon when Micah had his close encounter with death, he and Dana had just left the park after treating the crowd to a cringe-worthy round of knock-knock jokes, hood edition. The show featured such gems as:

Knock, knock.

Who's there?

Robin.

Robin, who?

Robbin' you. Hand over the cash.

Technically, the two friends were walking on the sidewalk, but every few steps, Micah would drop one foot off the curb and into the street and then bounce back up in an attempt to steal Dana's basketball.

"Missed again," Dana repeatedly taunted. "You can't touch this!"

As Dana paused at the busy intersection at 31st Street and Brooklyn Avenue to look both ways before crossing, Micah seized the opportunity. In a motion too swift for any driver to anticipate, he darted behind an enormous maple tree and stepped into the street—just as Cecil Jenkins' Fresh Fish Mobile rounded the corner. The sudden impact sent the startled child flying. Dana watched in horror as he landed with a thud on the opposite side of the street.

"Lay still, boy. I already called the ambulance," Mr. Cecil commanded in the familiar, raspy voice the kids joked about.

I wasn't even driving fast, he thought as he placed a smelly tarp around Micah's twisted leg. *The boy came out of nowhere. His poor momma gon' have a heart attack.*

Micah lay on his back, half-on, half-off the curb, confused by all the voices talking fast but making no sense. Although everyone seemed to be focused on his leg, it was his head that was in pain. Squinting against the sun, he searched the crowd. When he heard the sirens, he panicked, but not for himself. Where was Dana?

Please, Jesus, don't let her be hurt, he prayed.

Micah swallowed hard to clear his throat.

"Dana," he choked out. "Is Dana okay?"

"I'm here," Dana answered, pushing through the crowd.

Since witnessing her best friend go airborne, she had been cowering behind the tree, convinced Micah was dead.

"Thank God," she cried, parroting her mother's favorite affirmation when something awful turned out positive.

After what felt like forever, the first responders arrived, and the crowd dispersed. As the paramedics lifted Micah into the ambulance, he squeezed Dana's hand.

"Pray for me," he pleaded, tears in his eyes.

"What!?" Dana said. "How do I do *that?*"

"Coloring books...my room...under the Legos," Micah explained with a calm that defied the gravity of the situation. "Go tell my momma what happened, and then take 'em. Jesus will show you the way."

Soon afterward, the dynamic duo of Micah and Dana had morphed into the Three Musketeers: Micah, Dana...and Jesus Christ. Since the hospital only allowed family to visit, Dana turned to Micah's books for comfort. Each night before bed, she would choose a new image to color and circle any phrases she didn't understand. After 11 days, Micah came home with a four-inch scar on the back of his head and a compound fracture in his leg that would keep him bedridden for weeks.

"Guess what!?" he greeted Dana, all smiles, his wheelchair decked out in a bright Spiderman pattern. "Momma said we can have Bible study in my room."

With that, nearly every school night, right after Micah and Dana finished their homework, kiddie church was in session. At first, Ms. Sampson allowed Dana to visit for only a few minutes, just long enough for Dana and Micah to cover the parts she didn't understand. Once Micah was strong enough to sit up for longer periods, the two would stay in for hours, taking turns reading the stories aloud and dissecting their meaning.

"Just like the Deacon Charles and the old church ladies," Dana would tease.

Micah had already filled in most of the pictures, but Dana didn't care. She was more interested in the words. Plus, she was fascinated by how Micah could always connect the stories to real life. He used the story of Jesus healing ten lepers, with only one praising God afterward, to teach Dana about gratitude.

"No matter what, you gotta take the time to say 'thank you' to God and other people," Micah explained. And after learning about David and Goliath, Dana understood why Micah wasn't afraid after his accident.

"I have faith," he said. "God always takes care of me."

For the next seven years, Dana became Micah's Christian shadow, attending services at Ebenezer Baptist Church with his family. In the summer before middle school, she even joined him for a week at Bible camp in the scenic Ozark Mountains in southern Missouri.

As Dana entered her 20s, her worship attendance waned, but her faith held strong. In line with Baptist tradition, the when each of her sons turned one, she even "gave them back to God" as part of Ebenezer Church's baby dedication. And as soon as her babies could mimic words, she insisted they say their prayers before meals and at bedtime.

Since the year before her first child was born, Dana's favorite Sunday morning ritual had been to open her King James Bible and read aloud whatever Scripture God put in front of her.

Whatever happened to that girl?

Emboldened by memories of Micah's fighting spirit, Dana leaped to her feet, brushed the snow from her too-thin coat, and darted across the deserted street. What if she could go back and rediscover her faith? For her babies, her brothers and sisters. For herself.

Maybe God is not through with me yet, she hoped.

As if on cue, the yellow lamp in the sanctuary foyer switched from OFF to ON.

TWENTY EIGHT

Selfish or Self*less*

For a day—ok, for at least a few hours—Dana found rest on that cold ceramic tile in the homeless shelter lobby. Sometimes peace is a dangerous thing.

♥

"THERE'S STILL COFFEE, Ms. D, and half a turkey sandwich. Feels like you need to eat."

*H*ow does he do that—know exactly what I need before I know it myself? Dana thought, slamming the heavy steel door behind her.

Now feeling foolish for spending all night out in the cold, she stomped the snow off her frozen feet and made a beeline to the serving station behind the ushers' pews. Mackenzie Davis,

Ebenezer's senior pastor, was at the piano, Lemon Pledge in hand, wiping down the already-spotless surface. Pastor Mac—a nickname given him by the Young Adult Ministry—was a sizable man, six foot four and well over three hundred pounds. His chocolate skin, pearly white teeth, and customary black and white three-piece suit were reminiscent of a jazz musician in a 1920s speakeasy. Despite his girth, the humble leader possessed a gentle spirit that allowed him to glide through the world in unintimidating silence. But with that quiet came an awareness, an intuition—a sixth sense of sorts that, at first encounter, was difficult to understand. For Dana, the explanation was obvious: Pastor Mac was psychic.

Dana first suspected supernatural intervention during her first church visit, when she and Micah tried to sneak Legos into the Sunday school class. The giggly tweens were astounded when Pastor Mac busted them before a single toy was out of their pockets.

"Good morning, loves. Now, hand 'em over," he'd commanded in a booming but kind voice, with his large, navy-blue-tinted wireframe glasses pressed tightly against his forehead.

And years later, at Dana and Terran's wedding reception, when the head of the culinary ministry's son confessed that he'd forgotten the "baby cakes"—tiny vanilla cupcakes made especially for TJ and his cousins—it was Pastor Mac who'd solved the mystery before Dana blew a gasket.

"Are you sure, boy?" he'd asked calmly. "Why don't you go check your momma's car again? And this time, look good."

As predicted, the nervous courier found the small white box of treats in the trunk—in plain view—atop the spare tire. From unplanned pregnancies to extramarital affairs to embarrassing health issues, pretty much everyone in Ebenezer's tight-knit congregation accepted that trying to keep secrets from Pastor Mac was a losing proposition. The man saw *everything*; no minor feat since, thanks to a strategically placed landmine on a dimly lit road in Vietnam, Mackenzie Davis was legally blind.

Dana warmed her hands on the Styrofoam cup, took small sips of the powerful elixir, and waited. After a barely audible "Amen," the pastor turned off the podium light and headed for the last pew on the left. It had been more than a year since Dana had attended church services, but only two weeks since she and Pastor Mac had met in this exact spot, "rightly dividing the Word of Truth" (2 Timothy 2:15), he would tease.

"What does Ms. Sandy think about you hanging out at the church this late, Pastor?" Dana teased. "I know you're gettin' ready for tomorrow's Thanksgiving service, but don't you have to help cook?"

"Child, nobody wants me doin' no cooking," Mac chuckled. "Besides, if I was there, I wouldn't be here for you. Last time, we were talkin' 'bout being selfish. Is that still what's on your mind?"

Unbeknownst to Dana, Pastor Mac knew all about her recent trials. Just a few days earlier, he'd met, counseled, and prayed with

Terran and his new friend Tawana. The stories Terran had shared had made Pastor Mac's heartache, especially for all the children involved. Despite their lighthearted banter, seeing Dana in this state elevated his heartache to nearly heartbreak.

Earlier, when they'd hugged, Mac could feel Dana's rib bones through her coat and bulky sweater. And he couldn't help notice how her once-uninhibited laugh sounded forced. But what worried the pastor most was Dana's newfound obsession with altruism. When their late-night sessions began, it encouraged Mac that their studies of Scriptures, such as Romans 12:1 and Mark 10:45, seemed to inspire Dana to appreciate the virtues of putting others' needs ahead of one's own. But lately, as almost every conversation focused on death, Pastor Mac couldn't help but wonder if one of Ebenezer's most carefree souls might be searching for a reason to give up.

Tonight's conversation would do little to ease his fears.

"So, I was thinking about King Solomon and the dispute over a baby" (1 Kings 16), Dana began. "Solomon knew a true mother would rather give up her child than see him harmed."

"Yes, it's a lesson about sacrifice," Pastor Mac replied. "And about the infinite depths of a mother's love. There's nothing deeper, except God's love."

"I don't think I could live with the pain of having to give up my babies," Dana confessed so softly that Mac had to lean in to hear. "I would rather the king saw me in half. I know the Bible says there's no love greater than to lay down your life for a friend

(John 15:13). But what if you die to stop hurting people? Isn't that Christ-like?"

"Well, I can't argue with the Word," Pastor Mac responded cautiously. "But there's a difference between laying down your life and ending it. Only God has the right—and the *power*—to take a life."

Okay. Dana rested her head on the back of the pew. *But who's to say what or who God might use to wield that power?*

Sensing something was amiss, Mac adjusted his posture and reached for Dana's hand. But before he could say anything more, his wayward parishioner was on her feet.

"Can we pray now, Pastor?" she asked. "I need to go see my momma."

TWENTY NINE

Premonition

"BOY, YO' GRANDMA WOULD BE FREAKIN' OUT right about now."

Dana dabbed the freshly rolled joint against her coated tongue. It was Thanksgiving morning, so early you could still make out the shadow of the harvest moon through the petite windows in Momma D's basement. She and her 16-year-old nephew were sitting back to back under the snow-packed window wells. Dana had arrived at the side door hours earlier, sweaty and glassy-eyed, tapping incessantly and waking Damon with a start.

"You better not trip," she said.

"Chill, Auntie," Damon replied. "You act like this is my first time."

True, Dana and Damon had gotten high together before, but this was the first time they'd been so bold as to light up with his grandmother sleeping upstairs. As they took turns watching smoke rings float up and out the window, Dana wrapped the black and gold Mizzou blanket more tightly around her shoulders and marveled at how much her nephew had grown.

Damon Lee was the first and undisputed favorite grandchild of the Lawton clan. His mother, Casandra, had gotten pregnant by Ms. Mae's oldest son when she was only 17—the two became more than play cousins when Damon Sr. lived with the Lawtons at the start of his rebellious years. This charismatic figure with an irresistible smile lived fast and died young, shot seven times by a rival drug dealer when his son was only a toddler. Five years later, Casandra met Thomas, a kind, hardworking soul 20 years her senior, and moved her son to the suburbs just as he was entering puberty. At first, life in suburbia was good. Damon was an easygoing kid, sensitive and kind. Because he was an athlete— basketball was his passion—he had no trouble making friends in the mostly white middle school. For a teen mother, Casandra was strict, especially about her son's social life.

"Before I let these streets have my son," she would promise, "I'll take him out my *damn* self."

That's where Momma D came in. Damon was well aware of how much his grandma missed having him under her roof, and like any self-indulgent teenager, he wasn't above leveraging that fact to his advantage. Make no mistake—the boy genuinely enjoyed working in the yard, drinking sweet tea, and listening to old-school music with his grandma.

"She don't treat me like a baby," he would explain.

But it didn't hurt that her house was within walking distance of some of the best unsupervised house parties his old stomping grounds had to offer.

"Grandma needs me to cut her grass on Saturday," he'd announce, usually when Casandra and Thomas were distracted. "But y'all don't need to make a special trip; I can take the bus down there Friday after school and then ride home with y'all Sunday after dinner."

"Uh-huh," his mother would concede, only half-listening.

At Grandma's, as long as Damon didn't play his music too loud, finished his chores, and never missed breakfast, he could pretty much come and go as he pleased. If he bent the rules, his grandma might fuss a bit, but that would be it. But don't get it twisted—if Damon and Dana got caught doing what they were doing now, all hell would break loose.

As her fingertips began to warm, Dana snuffed out the joint, fanned away the last puffs of smoke, and closed the window.

"Auntie, I need to tell you something," he said, donning the demeanor of a much younger child. "Last week, I had a dream you died."

Surprised, Dana tried to lighten the mood.

"Boy, I told you not to trip," she joked.

But it was clear her nephew was not about to let this go. Even though he'd never seen her hit the pipe, he had older friends for whom the neighborhood crack houses were like second homes. The stories Damon had heard about his favorite aunt were embarrassing—and terrifying: fainting spells, seizures, group sex, and random shootings with little regard for innocents, even children, in the line of fire. Damon was high, but he wasn't trippin'. He *had* to make her listen.

"Please, Auntie," he warned. "Think of Terran and Tyler."

The mention of her boys' names hit a nerve. Dana's voice shook as she pulled her nephew close. Only God could use this sensitive child to break through the veneer of bravado that had enabled her to ignore the truth for so long.

"Terran and Tyler are *all* I think about," she answered, tears now streaming. "If it wasn't for them, I would have committed suicide a long time ago. But I could never force my kids to spend the rest of their lives explaining why their mother offed herself. There's a special place in hell for parents like that. My life sucks, and I don't see it getting better anytime soon. But I'm still trying. "

Damon exhaled and laid his head on Dana's lap.

"Good. That's good, Auntie," he said. "I'm just a kid, but I think it's okay that somebody else is the only reason you want to live, as long as you want to live."

THIRTY

Momma's House

S TAY OUT OF MY POT: words to live by for first-time guests at
a rave—and for any well-meaning but uninvited "helper" in
Momma Dana Lawton's kitchen.

Momma D approached Sunday afternoon meal preparation
with militaristic discipline. No matter the menu—an enormous pot
of spaghetti with garlic bread, smoked green beans, and German
chocolate cake one week; smothered pork chops, greens,
cornbread, and homemade sweet potato pie the next—the fare was
always delicious, abundant, and ready to serve by 3:00 p.m. The
playbook to achieve this weekly miracle existed only in Momma's
head—no recipe cards, no spreadsheets, not even a hastily
scribbled tally of the hordes of kids, grandkids, friends, and
neighbors likely to show up, mostly unannounced. Others

contributed—when ribs were on the menu, middle son Gregory was the de facto grill master, his 10 years as a chef at the family's favorite barbecue joint earning special privileges. And grandson Damon had shucked more corn and peeled more potatoes in his young life than many trained sous chefs. But no one, not even cooks many years Momma D's senior, dared to add a pinch of this or a drop of that without permission. *Momma didn't play that.*

For the Lawtons, the upcoming holiday was about more than a meal. As in years past, Thanksgiving was an opportunity to start over. Fact is, brothers fight, sisters squabble, and cousins cuss each other out. But on that day, no matter the weather or previous drama, folks came from near and far to break bread and wipe the slate clean, such was the power of Momma's invitation.

It was just after 6:00 a.m. on Thanksgiving morning, and Momma and Greg had been banging pots since dawn. An enormous roasted turkey, four fruit salads, five cakes, and at least 10 pies sat cooling on the windowsill. Rolls were rising, greens were washed, macaroni noodles were boiling, and an assortment of pork and beef ribs sat marinating in the overstuffed refrigerator.

Almost done, Momma D thought. *And the sun's up—time to take a break.*

She poured a cup of coffee, plopped down at the dining room table, and retrieved the phone from beneath a mountain of Black Friday sales ads.

"Hell-ooooo!" consummate middle child Lenita bellowed in her silliest, sing-song voice.

"Hello-baby-it's-your-mother," Momma responded without taking a breath.

Come on, Momma, I know your voice, Lenita thought, smiling. Still, the familiar, ridiculous exchange never got old.

"I know it's early and you probably workin' on your dinner, but I need you to bring me two nice tablecloths before it gets too late."

Already downstairs but still in her pajamas, Lenita flipped on the kitchen lights and ran her fingers across the marble countertops. "Really, Momma? Again with the tablecloths? Why on earth do y'all need replacements every year?"

"Guess somebody's eatin' 'em," Momma replied, laughing. "Don't fuss. Your homemade rolls will be ready when you get here."

"Okay. I'm on my way," Lenita relented, deciding it would be better to go now and get back before her own household came to life. Forty minutes later, she was standing in her mother's foyer, shaking snow off her down-filled coat as her nephew emerged from his basement lair.

"Hi, Auntie," Damon greeted her with a hug. "What 'chu doing here so early? You know dinner won't be ready before three."

"I know," Lenita scoffed. "Your Grandma needed tablecloths—*again.* Uncle Kenny and cousin Jess are here from Texas. Terran and Tyler are at Malia's. We'll be back around five to eat dessert and take the kids to see the holiday lights. Who knows where Auntie Dana is."

"She's downstairs, sleeping," Damon whispered so his grandma wouldn't hear. "Showed up this morning lookin' real scary."

"Thank you, Lord," Lenita gasped to Damon's surprise. "You tell her I need to talk to her. I gotta go."

THIRTY ONE

Oh, Give Thanks

A LOUD, AROMA-FILLED ASSAULT on the senses—that's what holiday revelers at the Lawtons expected, and Thanksgiving 1996 did not disappoint. While the official blessing of the food didn't occur until 3:00 p.m., the noise, noshing, and neighborly drop-bys started before noon and continued well into the night. Each year, between 30 and 40 guests—kids, grandkids, great-grandkids, cousins, friends, and friends of friends—trickled through the weather-worn oak door of the beige, three-story colonial to eat, drink and be merry at Momma D's table. If this was your first time, you couldn't help but notice the house was in desperate need of repair. And some of the life-scarred faces in the crowd might prompt you to keep a close eye on your valuables. But before long, somewhere between your second cup of spiked punch and the impromptu pre-teen talent show, anxiety would give way to admiration for your host and extreme gratitude to whoever had invited you.

That morning, Momma D's typical pre-meal anxiety was palpable, but deep down, she *loved* the crazy.

"Boy, you workin' my nerves," she snapped as Damon squeezed behind her to get milk from the refrigerator. "Hurry up with that cereal so you can put out the tablecloths and sweep the living room floor. I need to get the macaroni and cheese in the oven, or there won't be enough time to bake eight pans of rolls. Go ask Greg to put on some church music."

"Uncle Greg's outside at the grill, Grandma," Damon answered, careful not to introduce even a hint of sass into his tone. "I'll pick something, *not* hip-hop."

Except for the tablecloths, Momma's cornucopia of holiday ornamentation had been on full display for more than a week. In the large dining room—Thanksgiving Central—gaudy strands of gold lamé hung loosely from the half-lit chandelier and cherry-red armoire. Plastic red poinsettias, many adorned with bright silver bells, were positioned as centerpieces atop every flat surface: the main table and two dessert tables in the dining room, as well as the coffee table, end tables, and non-working floor-model television in the living room. Even the dusty family photos on the mantel above the fireplace dripped with fake snow.

Momma was so focused on keeping the cheese on her macaroni from bubbling over in the oven that she didn't hear the doorbell. No matter, as her youngest son, Roger (the family called him Rock), had no problem letting himself in. Hajji, Rock's younger cousin, a high-functioning alcoholic, trailed close behind.

Rock strolled into the kitchen without a sound and planted a kiss on his mother's sweaty cheek.

"Boy, you scared me!" she snapped.

Momma patted her brow with a flour-covered dish towel and turned to her nephew. Lips pursed, she scanned Hajji from head to toe.

"Hey, Day-oh," Hajji mumbled, using the nickname his mother, Gemma, had bestowed on her older sister when the two were kids, his eyes glued to his shoes to avoid the piercing stare.

"Lord help you, boy," Momma prayed aloud.

Here was her dead sister's child: six feet tall, not 125 pounds soaking wet, covered in day-old grime and reeking of cheap vodka.

"You know dinner won't be ready until three. Did you bring the paper plates and napkins?" she asked.

Rock gestured towards the two 60-count packages he'd already placed on the cramped kitchen counter.

"You know Muslims don't do holidays, Momma," he reminded her, stroking his chest-length beard. Rock had converted to Islam years earlier, after more than a decade in prison for (what else?) drug trafficking. His legal name was now Saed, but to his family, he would always be Rock.

"We're working today. Trying to catch up on that remodel on 35th Street. But that don't mean we can't eat. We'll come by later—after Hajji takes a bath," he teased. "Save me some yams."

As he approached the front door, Rock nearly collided with Dana, who was tiptoeing up the back stairs to sneak into the bathroom, brand-new toothbrush in hand. Before her brother could blurt out some snarky greeting, she pressed her index finger to her lips and shook her head back and forth, her eyes pleading.

"Shhh!"

When they were kids, Rock had taken pleasure in torturing his little sister, reporting her mischievous antics to Momma as soon as he became aware of them. Not anymore. Not today.

At the sight of her, Rock's smile faded, and he stretched out his arms. Surprised by her bratty brother's tenderness, Dana leaned in to welcome his embrace.

"I love you, sister," he said tenderly.

Dana smirked, planted a quick peck on her brother's scraggly cheek, and then skipped up the stairs.

That was the last time Rock would see his sister alive.

THIRTY TWO

Nobody Like Family

Ok, Dana. You've been trying to BS your way out of this for months. Today those chickens come home to roost.

♥

"AUNTIE DANA, AUNT MALIA SAID GET YO' BUTT UPSTAIRS or she's telling Grandma you here."

This was the third time Damon had popped his head through the basement door, his voice barely audible over the loud-talking adults, rambunctious children, and Z.Z. Hill's "Down Home Blues" reverberating through the floorboards.

Ok, time to face 'em. Dana had been dressing, if you could call it that, for hours. Her only decent outfit—a sleek black jumpsuit she'd boosted from Macy's a few weeks ago—was literally falling off her emaciated frame. Her hair was in an up-do, the only style capable of hiding the bald spots. Weeks ago, the crack-induced scabs had fallen from her face, but her cheap makeup did little to hide the scars. *This is as good as it gets,* she thought.

Snuffing out the last of her joint, Dana pulled on her bright red ankle boots, flashed the biggest smile she could muster, and bounded up the stairs.

Momma's basement door opened into the high-traffic foyer between the kitchen and the living room. Sensing the coast was clear, Dana cracked the door and stepped out, taking care not to collide with any of the fast-moving toddlers. As (bad) luck would have it, Momma chose that exact moment to sneak in a much-needed bathroom break. As their eyes met across the foyer, the two Danas froze. Though she hadn't seen her daughter for months, Momma D had spoken to Dana on the phone only a few weeks ago. Nothing in that conversation had prepared her for what she was seeing today.

"Lord Jesus," Momma gasped. "The folks over at the Multi-Purpose Center tried to tell me you were in a bad way, but I didn't want to believe it. Girl, you look like death on a soda cracker! You need help, baby. Why don't you stay here tonight, and I'll take you to the rehab center myself first thing tomorrow morning?"

Before Dana could answer, a horde of little hands attacked her, wrapping themselves around her legs, nearly knocking her off her feet.

"Momma!" TJ and Tyler squealed.

"Auntie, come play with us," niece Ashley and nephew Alex coaxed, each pulling her in opposite directions.

"My babies," Dana responded, laughing out loud for the first time in days and allowing the kids to drag her away.

"I'm ok, Momma. Just lost some weight," she replied before returning her attention to the children. "Come on, y'all, let's eat."

As the kids led her to the buffet line, Dana steeled herself for the verbal firing squad her mercilessly blunt sisters, brothers, cousins, and friends were about to unleash. She expected sarcasm—that was the Lawton way of dealing with stress. But what she hadn't expected was the genuine fear in the eyes of those she loved.

"Hey, I see you're on that crackhead diet," sister Rayna started. "You might want to ease up a bit."

"Looks like you forgot something when you got dressed this morning," oldest sister Casandra said. "Where's your butt?"

"How was the baseball game?" Lenita asked with a snort. "Thanks for letting me know you weren't dead."

"Y'all are hilarious." Dana laughed, pretending to ignore their questions as she coaxed baby Tyler back to the table to finish his green beans. "What y'all need to do is stop trippin'. I got this."

"Yeah, right," Cousin Charles replied. For years, he'd been watching his younger brother Hajji headed down the same path. "You keep telling yourself that."

After a serious, rapid-fire interrogation about Terran's new girlfriend (Malia had brought everyone up to speed), Thanksgiving dinner went off without a hitch. Though Dana was surrounded by some of the most judgmental people she knew, more than anywhere else, for the first time in a long time, she felt safe. In a weird way, she was relieved everything was now out in the open. For the rest of the evening, conversations seesawed from whose kid had done the weirdest thing lately to what was on everyone's Christmas list, with a few "crack is whack" jabs thrown in for good measure. The consummate clown, Dana rolled her eyes and cracked jokes to deflect attention. Through it all, Momma D sat at the head of the table, sipping sweet wine, not speaking, watching her youngest daughter like a hawk. The signs were clear: pupils dilated, sweating, absentmindedly scratching her arms and legs. Her daughter needed a hit, and there was nothing Momma D could do to stop her from trying to get one.

As the mothers served the last of the sweet potato pie, the littlest Lawtons were getting restless.

"Listen up," Malia announced. "Time to load up to go see the holiday lights. Little people, get your coats on, and we can decide who's riding with whom when we get outside."

Kids cheered. Adults groaned.

"I'm staying with Momma," TJ announced definitively.

Dana's oldest son's clinginess was uncharacteristic for his age, but understandable. The boy had been burned so many times before by his mother's "I'll be right back" disappearing act that tonight, he was determined not to let her out of his sight.

As the adults gathered in the kitchen to make to-go plates, one by one, Dana planted wet kisses on each little person's forehead as she fastened their coats. When it was TJ and Tyler's turns, she scooped both of them up in her arms and hugged them way too tightly.

"Can't breathe!" Tyler protested.

"Momma's sorry," Dana teased, tickling his ears. "I just love y'all so much. Y'all know that, right?"

TJ nodded as Tyler wiggled out of his mother's grasp, eager to get on with the holiday adventure.

"Terran Jr., go over to the dessert table and get cookies for you and your brother," Dana instructed. "I need to go to the bathroom."

"Okay, Momma," TJ responded suspiciously. "I'll be right over there when you come back downstairs."

"Cookie!" Tyler squealed, pushing his brother aside.

Her boys now distracted, Dana headed toward the stairs. Instead of going up, she detoured down to the basement and closed the door. She donned her coat, hat, and scarf, pausing once to listen for protests. Willing herself not to cry, she took one last look around the familiar makeshift bedroom, grabbed her purse, and let herself out the side door.

Impulse control, perhaps, could be the most consequential virtue one loses to addiction. As Dana stepped off the porch, the brisk winter air slapped her across the face. A light snow was falling, just enough to shroud the streetlights in an eerie white gauze. After walking only a few blocks, the muscles in Dana's legs began to throb. Her ears were numb, and the tips of her fingers tingled through thin pleather gloves. Physically, her body itched with the familiar ache of being in full tweak mode. Emotionally, what she was experiencing was more complex. Suddenly a flood of memories and emotions—shame, sadness, and abject terror—coursed through the chronic jokester's frail body with such intensity she had to stop to catch her breath. It was one thing to duck out on her children, as trifling as that was. But what she'd done at MJ's a few days earlier, well, that was just plain stupid. And dangerous.

THIRTY THREE

Friends, Conditionally

Momma always told us God could use anyone to fulfill His will. Well,
apparently, so can Satan.

♥

ADDICTION MAKES STRANGE BEDFELLOWS, but one thing
Dana had learned early on was that drugs and friendship do
not mix. No one can deny that getting high together, throwing
inhibitions to the wind, revealing innermost secrets, and swapping
spit with someone through a blue-hot glass pipe gives rise to a
level of intimacy most newlyweds only dream about. But then the
party ends, and what felt like genuine affection morphs into all-out
resentment. Lying begins, schemes hatch, sometimes violence
ensues, and you find yourself alone, embarrassed to admit you

breathe the same air as such a vile human being. The problem is that smoking crack alone can be deadly; you need someone to watch your back, especially if you're still trying to maintain a life. Enter the Friendly Enabler: a trusted user you knew from before—someone who cared enough not to push, but who welcomed you into this new mind-fried reality with open arms. Two such people from Dana's past had been all too quick to embrace this unscrupulous assignment: her sister/cousin Tina and Terry John Wallace.

Dana had met Terry Wallace, a wet-and-dry ice delivery man, a year earlier by accident. In fact, it's accurate to say the two literally *fell* into a friendship. The encounter occurred in the parking lot at Benton Liquors, blocks from Dana's home and, poetically, across the street from the infamous 27th Street bus stop. In this mostly black neighborhood, you would think a freakishly tall blond cowboy with steel-blue eyes would attract all kinds of attention—but not Terry. In brightly painted boots and a worn black hat, this guy was so obviously comfortable in his surroundings that the locals didn't give him a second look.

One warm Saturday, as Dana ran into the store for old-married-couple-date provisions—cheese, strawberries, crackers, and assorted adult beverages—and Terry hurried out, head down, a five-pound bag of ice on each shoulder, the two collided.

"Watch out, Iceman!" Dana snapped, clutching the glass Bacardi bottle to her chest as the other contents of her bag spilled onto the pavement.

"Sorry, suga' momma," Terry replied with a toothy grin. "If I'd seen yo' fine ass comin' this way, I gar-rawn-tee I woulda' been more careful."

Dana laughed out loud as this crazy white man helped her retrieve her purchases. *I like him,* she decided, flashing the sarcastic smile that endeared her to everyone she met.

From that day forward, the two frequently exchanged pleasantries, sometimes inside the store, but more often in the parking lot as Terry loaded and unloaded his wares. It would be much later, several months "A.C." (After Crack), that Dana would learn just how well the hastily ascribed nickname suited her new pal.

One chilly Monday morning, around 7:00 a.m., the witching hour when street dealers make themselves scarce—too much traffic—Dana was languishing at the 27th Street bus stop, trying to figure out how to score with no money. As she was about to get in the car with the first person to offer a quick fix, a deep Southern voice beckoned.

"Hey, suga' momma," Iceman yelled from across the street, "why don't y'all come on in out' the cold."

Though they'd been exchanging clever banter for more than a year, this would be Dana's first venture inside the faded green van. The vehicle's cargo area was roomier than expected. One side housed two industrial-sized freezers, and on the other rested a giant leather sofa. At first, the two sat in silence, sharing rum-spiked coffee from a silver thermos. Then, as a gust of wind whistled through the van's back doors, Terry retrieved a brand-new crack pipe from one of the freezers, two pasty-white rocks already inside.

"Iceman." He smirked. "Bet'chu didn't know I been watching. You and yo' cousin take a lot of chances. Next time you need somewhere to burn, hit me up. I know a place that's safe."

True to his word, Terry introduced Dana to a drug house far superior to any she'd seen. The place was located south of the city, in a quiet, well-cared-for neighborhood. From the neatly manicured lawn to the guest bathroom that reeked of Pine-Sol to the abundance of ashtrays throughout, it was obvious someone here cared about the details. After a dozen or so chaperoned visits, the exclusive establishment for discerning junkies known as the Ritz became Dana's go-to spot. She would later learn that the proprietor, a fair-skinned, impeccably dressed middle-aged brother named Michael James Alston, was one of Terry's oldest friends, or at least that's what it looked like.

"Acquaintance," Terry had corrected her. "NOT friend."

From the stories Dana had heard, it was clear these men had established a personal relationship well before either had entered the drug trade.

If, in Terry's mind, MJ didn't qualify as a friend, what did that say about her?

THIRTY FOUR

We Got History

"YOU NEED TO GET HER HERE, DEAD OR ALIVE."

Terry Wallace crouched just inside the crack house door, shifting from one foot to the other. He didn't need this shit. It was Thanksgiving morning; he had just made his last delivery of the night. He'd planned to stop by MJ's for only a moment to settle receipts and then have a quick hit to get him through what was sure to be a fucked-up brunch with his new girlfriend's family. Now here he was, watching a pissed-off psychopath twirl his familiar silver and black Glock .45 9mm, blaming him for something he knew nothing about.

"Remember that caramel-colored ho you vouched for? The bitch burned me last night," MJ ranted. "Slithered in here all sexy with that baseball player and then pulled a snatch and dash. Got cash, weed, rocks, the works. That shit *cannot* be tolerated, especially so soon after that asshole Monte's daddy paid me to give his boy a pass. So, here's the deal: *you* help us take care of *her*, or *we* take care of *you*."

Damn, suga' momma, Terry thought. *What have you done?*

He sidled up to the table, careful not to make any moves that could be interpreted as threatening. He removed his hat, dabbed his sweaty brow with his American flag handkerchief, and contemplated the last time he'd seen MJ so angry. That time, more than five years ago, there had been a girl at the center of that drama, too.

In 1989, Lieutenant Michael James Alston had just moved from the small town of Tarkio, Missouri, to Kansas City to join a new state-run Narcotics Task Force. Tired of being a big fish in a small pond, the seven-year police veteran had lobbied hard to convince his wife and teenage daughter that *this* move would make all their dreams come true.

Around the same time, Terry Wallace, a gangly redneck six years MJ's junior, was a few months into his job as a driver for Santolli's delivery service. Fate brought the men together, but it was fish that sealed the friendship.

"Hey, man, that accent—where are you from?" Mickey had asked the displaced cowboy in line ahead of him at his new favorite restaurant.

They were at City Fresh Sushi, a tiny seafood cafe across from the midtown police station. Mickey had been headed toward the second cashier, the soy-sauce-covered menu obstructing his view, when the voice had stopped him in his tracks.

"Well," Terry replied, giving the nosy policeman the once-over, "My parents are from Oklahoma, but I was born and raised just north of here in a lil' ol' town called Rock Port. Bet you ain't heard of it."

"You'd lose that bet." Mickey laughed. "I'd recognize that twang anywhere! I'm from Tarkio. I moved here with the family a few months ago. Nice to see another highfalutin' hick make it out."

"Highfalutin'?" Terry chuckled. "Well, I guess it takes one to know one."

Since Terry's deliveries brought him to the café at least three times a week and Mickey was a sushi junkie, the guys were always running into each other. Soon the Northern Missouri homeboys realized they shared more than vocal intonation; both their fathers had worked for the Water Plant, and Mickey had played basketball with Terry's older cousin Jacob.

After weeks of listening to her husband recount all the colorful ways his new friend butchered the English language, Mickey's wife, Maya, began pressuring MJ to invite Terry to dinner.

"I don't care what color he is," Maya countered when her husband hinted that his new team might question what their boss could possibly have in common with a backwoods redneck.

"He's a fellow country boy, alone in the city. The least we can do is give him a home-cooked meal."

Mickey wasn't the only one with reservations about getting too close, but for reasons that had nothing to do with skin color. The last person Terry needed snooping around his life was a cop. Terry's employer, Nico Santolli, had a reputation for serving more than cold, dead fish to a select clientele. Since his second week on the job, at 5:00 a.m. each Thursday morning, Terry and two other drivers sat in their refrigerated vans, eyes front, as the Santolli grandsons loaded sealed metal containers into specially designed drawers beneath the custom freezers. Sometimes, when on break, the other drivers would brag about what they'd spied in the day's load—a kilo of heroin, three one-inch cartons of flawless diamonds, a hundred grand in cash. Not Terry. He enjoyed this job, and the off-the-books bonuses each month were nothing to scoff at. Terry also valued his freedom.

"I deliver fish," he'd tell anyone who tried to pull him into the conversation. "Anything else is none of my business."

Terry apologized more than a few times when Maya answered MJ's phone and asked him over for dinner, catching him off guard, "That's so sweet, but my work schedule is crazy this week. Maybe another time."

One Easter—the one day of the year when Santolli's shut down for Mass—Terry finally ran out of excuses.

"It's the Lord's day. You gotta eat," Maya scolded. "Don't make me call your Momma."

Terry relented, and to his surprise, after only half an hour at MJ's, he was having a blast. MJ's wife and teenage daughter, Nyla, were such sweethearts. Plus, the food was delicious: baked ham, fried catfish, sautéed spinach, glazed carrots, and peach cobbler. Since Maya didn't allow work talk at the dinner table, the conversation vacillated between goings-on back home, church work, and how Nyla was handling the move. The girl was petite for a 16-year-old, with striking features, coal-black eyes, and an awareness of fine cuisine the likes of which Terry had never seen in someone so young. Given this was her first time living in the big city, you might expect the five-foot-three Nyla to be subdued. You would be wrong.

"Honey, please, our Nyla's doing just fine," her mother interrupted with a playful eye roll. "She's taken over the cheerleading squad. And the girl asks so many questions, Sister Robinson recruited her to teach the young-adult Sunday school class at the church."

The accuracy of her mother's characterization caused Nyla to laugh so hard she nearly spat out her iced tea. "Momma, please," she said with a sigh, breathlessly clutching her imaginary pearls. "I can't help it. It's hard to contain all this fabulousness in such a small package."

Upon learning that Terry made deliveries to restaurants *and* that he liked sushi as much as her father, the young foodie launched into an interrogation that set her startled houseguest back on his heels.

"So, everyone's always talking about Kansas City steaks. What I want to know is who around here serves the best blackened salmon? Where can you find the freshest lobster? And do you trust the spring rolls at that little hole-in-the-wall deli on 18th Street? The snooty white kids at my school gobble them up like candy."

"Whoa, girl," Terry protested. "I only deliver the meat. But I hear things. And I've scored sample meals from about every four-star restaurant in the city. If you give me a break tonight *and* play your cards right, I might hook you up."

And hook her up, he did.

Back then, the Wallace-Alston relationship had been uncomplicated. The guys shared a meal a few times a week at City Fresh or another hot spot, or sometimes at Mickey's home. Small talk soon gave way to more personal and substantive exchanges: Terry's latest romantic conquest, how Mickey's daughter liked that new oyster bar, and, of course, who was doing whom back in Rock Port and Tarkio. Terry had a standing invitation to holiday celebrations. And more than a few times, after spotting Nyla hanging with friends at that 18th Street deli a little too close to curfew, he'd even given his adopted little sister a ride home. Back then, Terry reminisced, Mickey had been the closest thing to a friend he'd ever had. Funny how time flies.

Back in the crack house kitchen, Terry reared back in his chair, mesmerized by the angry vein pulsating on the side of Mickey's head. For the life of him, he couldn't understand why this dude was so freaked out. Before, dealing with a junkie who'd broken the rules, what the crack house sentries called "taking out the trash," had never bothered MJ. What about this contract had him so rattled?

Suddenly the reason for the over-the-top angst was so clear...and heartbreaking. In the past few months, MJ had gotten to know Dana—her quick wit, her love of family and faith, and how quickly this drug had obliterated her once blissfully ordinary life. The consummate bad guy had slipped up and allowed this troubled young woman to get into his head. Without ever knowing it, Dana had awakened a part of MJ that he thought he'd buried long ago.

Dang, Terry thought. *Dana reminds MJ of Nyla.*

THIRTY FIVE

Not My Baby

"HEY, MAN, HAVE YOU SEEN MY BABY GIRL out and about lately?"

The question was innocent enough, but something in this overprotective dad's tone warned Terry to temper his response. It was a work night, Thursday, well after 8:00 p.m. The men had commandeered the two front bar stools at Johnny's, a hole-in-the-wall beer and burger joint downtown, to celebrate Mickey's promotion to captain after only two years on the job. Hoping to lighten the mood, Terry flashed his signature smirk and took an extra-long swig of some new pale ale whose name he was now too drunk to pronounce.

"Dude, you tryna turn me into a spy?" he joked. "I *see* Nyla when I'm out making my rounds, sometimes at the sushi place, mostly behind Santolli's at the end of her part-time shift. But I ain't looking for her, and I'd like to keep it that way."

"Naw man," Mickey replied, brushing Terry off. "The wife made me ask. She's worried that something's not right since my girl broke up with her boyfriend."

With zero fanfare, last week, on her 18th birthday, Nyla had announced she'd selected a college—Fisk University—*and* ended her 13-month romance with high school classmate and star basketball forward Anthony "T-John" St. John. To Mickey, this was *not* breaking news. Nyla was headed to Nashville, while T-John was all set to attend Kansas University on scholarship. So, when his daughter missed curfew for the first time in her young life, he attributed the lightweight rebellion to "senioritis." His wife was convinced something else was going on.

"Thanks, man." He chuckled, clicking bottles with his friend. "I'll get Maya in check. She just needs to chill."

"Women," Terry teased. "Can't live with 'em, can't lock 'em in a shed out by the fish pond. I need to take a leak."

Terry retired to the men's room, and Mickey downed the last swallow of ale and signaled for the check. As he retrieved his wallet, his handheld radio crackled.

"Captain Alston, this is Reynolds at Dispatch," a familiar voice announced. "Be aware, units responding, 10-67, your residence."

Mickey froze. A 10-67 was code for CALL FOR HELP. At his *residence?*

"Say again," he barked, steadying himself against the bar stool.

"Ten-four. Any additional information?"

"Negative," Reynolds responded. "I suggest you call your wife."

Stumbling out the restroom door, Terry nearly collided with Mickey as he was hanging up the restaurant's payphone.

"Dispatch called. Something's up at my house. I tried calling, but no one's answering," Mickey spat. "Squad's on the way to pick me up. You should get a cab."

From there, the situation progressed from odd to bad to so much worse. When Mickey got home, Maya wasn't there, but his neighbor Gail greeted him at his front door, her face ashen.

"It's Nyla," she announced, blinking rapidly to hold back tears. "Some friends brought her home about a half-hour ago, eyes glassy, sweating, and foaming at the mouth. It looked like some kind of seizure. Maya called 911, told them she was your wife, and then left in the ambulance with Nyla—said Dispatch would locate you quicker than she could. Get there, Mickey. You need to get there now."

The emergency room at St. Mary's Hospital was eerily quiet until Dasia and Nina saw their best friend's father enter through the automatic glass doors.

"We're so sorry, Mr. Alston," the girls blurted out simultaneously, cheap mascara running down their faces. "We didn't know. *Nobody* knew."

Mickey's heart was beating a mile a minute, but by tapping into techniques learned at last fall's crisis intervention training, he was able to will himself to project complete calm.

"Focus!" he bellowed louder than intended. "Where's my family?"

This time, Nina, the taller of the two, was the only one to speak. Swallowing hard, she explained that doctors had moved Nyla to a special intensive care unit on the fourth floor—only family allowed. With that, Mickey took off so abruptly the girls had to run to keep up.

"When they kicked us out, the doctors were covering her with ice packs and sticking needles in her arms," Nina cried.

In the elevator, as both girls again spoke at once, Mickey struggled to process what he was hearing. Graduation party at a dude named Jack Thompson's house. Nyla walks in on T-John banging some cheerleader over the bathroom sink. She runs down the stairs and out the back door to "get some air." Thirty minutes later, Nina and Dasia find their one-woman anti-drug campaign drooling on the concrete floor in the Thompson's garage, a heroine-laced needle in her lap.

"Mr. Alston, the doctors say Nyla OD'd!" Nina screamed. "We couldn't believe it."

Apparently, the amicable break-up story Nyla had relayed to her parents had been a ruse. The couple hadn't mutually agreed to "just be friends" so they could focus on college. T-John had unceremoniously dumped Nyla, calling her a prudish bitch in front of everyone after she'd chastised him for using steroids.

Never one to debase herself publicly, Nyla had flashed that million-dollar smile. "Just say no," she'd responded sarcastically, high-fiving her girls in self-congratulatory delight. Privately, though, this critique from the first guy she'd ever loved had shaken her, compelling her to question everything she thought she knew about what it means to be a strong, independent, and *fearless* woman. It was these new insecurities, stoked by an ill-timed "I dare you" from some resident stoners huddled on the Thompson's back porch as Nyla had run by, that had set in motion the perfect storm her family was embroiled in today.

When the elevator doors opened to the fourth floor, a rush of anxiety washed over Mickey. As they approached the nurse's station, he and the terrified teens could hear the unmistakable cries of someone in pain.

"May I help you?" a pale, dwarf-sized male nurse asked matter-of-factly.

No one heard him, though, as the drama playing out over the man's head was consuming all their attention. In a small, glass-enclosed room, two white-coated doctors, an elderly nurse, and three uniformed police officers were kneeling in a circle. At the center was Maya, Mickey's usually poised and proper wife. She was laying on her side, hair askew, hands over her ears, screaming at the top of her lungs. As if on cue, she lifted her head as Mickey opened the door. Their eyes met, and he knew: Nyla was dead.

The rest of the evening was a blur. After nearly two hours of tears, rants, and interrogation, the police backed off, leaving their fellow officer to grieve. The girls offered their friend's parents a ride, but after all that Maya had been through, Mickey could not subject her to Nina's 1982 Toyota Corolla two-door with the questionable heater and cracked windshield. Doctors prescribed Maya a mild sedative, and she departed for home in the same squad car that had delivered her husband to that godforsaken scene hours earlier.

Over the next few weeks, while his wife planned their daughter's funeral, Mickey plotted revenge. According to his partner on the Narcotics task force, the night Nyla had died, six other teens had shown up in emergency rooms across the city with similar symptoms. Apparently, someone had put out a batch of heroin cut with the deadly synthetic opioid Fentanyl. Officers surmised that the reason Nyla was the only one who lost her life was her lack of experience and unfamiliarity with the signs of overdose. Not surprisingly, none of the survivors would speak directly to authorities, but an anonymous tip had already led the cops to the source: a well-known dealer who worked out of a rundown apartment building north of the low-income housing project on Fifth Street. Two weeks later, that house mysteriously burned to the ground with two dealers barricaded inside. The following Monday, newly minted KCPD Captain Michael Alston announced his early retirement. Nyla's case was officially closed, but her father's transition from decorated crime fighter to hardened criminal was just beginning. Considering it had taken 10 years to achieve all he was about to abandon, Mickey's descent was swift and systematic.

The first step: *Eliminate from your life anything capable of inducing heartache.*

For weeks after his daughter's death, Mickey used excessive drinking, heavy weed smoking, and dalliances with known crack whores to pretty much destroy all of his professional relationships, including longtime partnerships in law enforcement. And as his grief morphed into rage, he became so abusive that his loved ones were forced to retreat for their own safety.

"You were her mother!" he repeatedly lashed out at Maya, weapon in hand. "You knew she was suffering. Why didn't you do something?!"

One especially scary night, he even threatened Terry at gunpoint. The two were leaving Santolli's, Nyla's favorite restaurant, after a relatively pleasant night of dinner and drinks. Terry *thought* the evening had been cathartic, but as they crossed the empty parking lot to retrieve their cars, Mickey stopped in his tracks.

"What's up, bro? You too drunk to drive?" Terry joked.

With unexpected swiftness, Mickey grabbed his friend by the neck and pressed the Glock to Terry's chin.

"Some friend you are," he said, tears flowing. "Did you ever wonder why no cops ever showed up at the dock where you work? The guys heard rumors about those ice vans, but I convinced them not to waste their time. I covered for *you*. You failed *her*."

After seven months of threatening, crying, and praying, Maya filed for divorce and moved back to Tarkio. Terry also severed ties, and he even shared Mickey's revelation with Mr. Santolli, abandoning his "don't see nothing, don't say nothing" approach to life. Turns out, the old man was a step ahead of him.

"Thanks for the tip," he told Terry. "But don't sweat it. We have insurance—friends in the mayor's office."

In appreciation for his loyalty, Santolli offered Terry a promotion: lead driver, bigger tips, and freedom to use the van when he was off the clock to run his own routes. It took Terry about 30 seconds to accept.

Principles be damned, he reasoned. *Life's short. Look what happened to Nyla.*

It's safe to assume the Mickey-Terry brotherhood would have remained in the past had it not been for Lola, the abandoned progeny of one of Mickey's no-name affairs. Suddenly he had a daughter again. The child had needs, her father was a rage-filled alcoholic whose career was no more, and her mother was nowhere to be found. Mickey needed another plan.

The outreach occurred two years to the day after the Nyla catastrophe. To anyone listening, the exchange sounded like nothing more than two business associates negotiating a deal.

Terry answered the phone on the first ring. "Hey."

"Hey," Mickey responded flatly. "You still drivin' that van? I have a proposition."

The offer was a partnership. In exchange for a cut of the earnings, Terry would provide exclusive pickup and delivery services for Mickey's new venture: the Ritz.

Rest in peace, Captain Alston.

Hello, MJ, drug czar.

THIRTY SIX

The Iceman Cometh

NOWHERE TO GO.

The realization landed as rapidly as the fat, wet snowflakes atop Dana's frozen toes. Since pulling off the Thanksgiving Evening Great Escape, she'd been meandering through the streets, first east, then south, then east again, her clothes soaked with sweat despite the sub-zero temperatures. She needed to score fast, but where?

The 27th Street bus stop was deserted. *Apparently, drug dealers take holidays, too.* And not only was Terran's spot still on Dana's no-fly list, but word on the street was that a dirty cop had put the place on lockdown after Landon had missed a few under-the-table payments.

With MJ's now off-limits, Dana was running out of options. Frustrated, she turned the corner at Benton Boulevard and looked north. Like a beacon on a hill, there, in the parking lot behind the liquor store, sat the familiar green van, engine running. Though the biting wind caused her eyes to water, Dana immediately recognized the hooded figure in the driver's seat, puffing on a cigarette: *Ice, Ice, Baby.* She grinned.

As Ice watched Dana draw closer, all smiles, his heart sank. He'd been in the game for a while. This wasn't his first clean-up. But he'd hoped the search for his friend-turned-target would take longer, especially since, truth be told, he hadn't been looking that hard. But like his crackhead sister often said: *Trouble always seems to find yo' address.*

Dana reached the van's cargo doors just as Ice released the lock from the inside. She pushed past him and, in a single motion, grabbed his thermos and plopped down on the sofa.

"It's colder than a motherfucker out there," she hissed.

"Yeah," Ice replied, "but word on the street is your ass is hot as hell."

"MJ," Dana acknowledged, avoiding eye contact. "I know. My life is officially FUBAR: fucked up beyond all recognition. So what the hell. Let's get high."

"I got 'chu," Ice teased in his best Wanda from *In Living Color* voice. He directed Dana toward a built-in metal toolbox between the two ice coolers. Inside were two already-filled crack pipes.

"Fire it up," he directed. "I'll drive."

As her nerve endings tingled, Dana lay back and stared at the ceiling. She loved getting high in Ice's van. He usually headed for the interstate so he could drive fast in one direction to replicate the sensation of flying. This ride was different. Since Ice had covered the cargo area windows in black film, Dana couldn't be sure, but it didn't feel as if they were speeding, and he was taking a lot of turns. *Whatever,* she thought. Still, the radio was especially loud, even for Ice, who loved to play old-school rap music on blast. Her driver also seemed uncharacteristically quiet. And he hadn't once signaled her to pass the pipe.

"You can drop me on 35th near the gas station," she requested, eyes closed. She felt the van slow and then leave the pavement. Ice turned down the radio and shifted in his seat to look her in the eyes; he owed her that much.

"Sorry, suga' momma," he said. "You're a real fine lady. But I brought you in. That makes *yo'* shit *my* shit. You're smart. And sexy as hell. Maybe you can talk MJ out of it."

Confused, Dana sat up so she could look past Ice's emotionless face to the front windshield. Somehow they had ended up at the entrance to the alley: *MJ's* alley!

Panicked, Dana grabbed the metal bat Ice kept under the sofa for emergencies and swung as hard as she could. The tip of the weapon caught her deceitful chauffeur just above his right eye. As Ice slumped forward, Dana rolled off the couch, threw all 120 pounds of her scrawny frame against the back doors, and frantically yanked the handles. She could hear Ice muttering profanities while he struggled to regain his footing. As he braced himself between the center console to steady his aim, to his surprise, Dana stopped struggling and fell to her knees. Her hesitation was brief, only a few seconds, but that was all the experienced marksman needed.

Three bullets from a .38 Special tore through Dana's body like a hot knife through butter—two in the back, one in the head— propelling her through the back doors. TJ and Tyler's momma was dead before her face hit the pavement.

With his friend's feet still resting on the van's bumper, Ice put the vehicle in drive and lurched forward, causing the rest of Dana's body to spill out onto the gravel road.

Ice dialed up the volume on the radio and pulled away.

Oh well, she shouldn't have tried to run.

At the end of the alley, he paused, fired up a joint, and eased onto the quiet street, careful to avoid the ever-present puddle of sludge that oozed from the dumpster behind Mac's Barbecue Shack.

"Yuck," he said, wincing. "I hate that smell."

Cold. As. Ice.

THIRTY SEVEN

Could've Been Me

IT WAS AFTER MIDNIGHT, New Year's Day, 1997. A few months had passed since a sanitation worker had made the gruesome discovery on "Crackhead Row," the police nickname for MJ's alley. Tonight was bitterly cold, but not enough to deter revelers from firing off round after round of celebratory gunfire— and not enough to keep two skeletal addicts from paying their respects to a fallen sister.

"I TOLD YOU it was blood." Tina winced, wiping her stained thumb and forefinger on the frozen grass.

"Ugh," Janae coughed, her warm breath forming clouds in the bone-chilling air. "That's messed up. They coulda cleaned up better. For D."

The ladies were adorned in layers à la Salvation Army Chic: four hats, five sweaters, three skirts, and a mishmash of leggings, wool socks, and worn-out sneakers between them. Because money was tight (only enough for one dime rock), Tina and Janae had walked the eight blocks to the Ritz from Ms. Ruby's flophouse, where the two shared three plastic storage containers and a twin-sized bed. Since the night Dana had died, Janae had gone out of her way to avoid this end of the alley. *That coulda been me,* she had confessed during more than one drug-addled rant.

Not so for Tina. Since that fateful Thanksgiving evening, she had visited the scene of the crime more than half a dozen times with various members of Dana's family. Because some held Tina at least partially responsible for Dana's downfall, the Lawtons had all but forced their wayward cousin into the role of liaison between the official police report and what sources on the street said *really* happened. Hell, had she not passed out and arrived late for dinner at Momma D's that night, Tina probably would have been an eyewitness.

As is typical of crimes in the hood, the police investigation was swift and ineffectual. Since no one saw anything (yeah, right), leads were sparse. A single bullet recovered at the scene matched those used in three other crimes, for which no weapon had been found. Thanks to an "anonymous" tip compiled from facts Tina had seduced out of one of the sentries, the police had at least questioned Iceman and MJ. Both had ironclad alibis. Given the coroner's timeline, they had to have been in the house when the shooting took place, but so were 15 other friends and family members, including kids. Witnesses.

"For real, officer," MJ swore. "It was Thanksgiving. The house was packed. We didn't hear a thing."

Regardless of how intently she tried to steel herself, Tina was woefully unprepared for the tsunami of vitriol spewed upon her after Dana's death. While the sisters masked their jabs in sarcasm, Dana's mother was openly hostile, peppering her niece with hateful accusations as soon as she stepped into the Lawton kitchen to offer condolences. Most of the family blamed outsiders—the dealer, the scum who pulled the trigger, or the police for ignoring neighbors' tips about the known drug house. But in Ms. Dana's mind, Tina was the one person who had watched, hell, maybe even helped her youngest daughter to go astray. As far as she was concerned, Dana's blood was on her hands.

"My baby trusted you. Now she's dead," she'd barked coldly. "Your mother would be ashamed of you right now."

The words cut deeply, likely because, deep down, Tina knew Ms. Dana was right. Years earlier, Tina's proud, no-nonsense mother had died of lung cancer three days before her 38th birthday. When her sister-friend became ill, Ms. Dana had almost immediately, all but adopted Ms. Mae's children, connecting them to much-needed social services, extending open invitations to Sunday and holiday dinners, and getting after them, sometimes physically, when they got into trouble. Like Ms. Mae, Ms. Dana believed in disciplining with a strong hand.

"Spare the rod, spoil the child," the young mothers would announce before spankings. Some good *that* did.

At the dining room table, head in hand, studying headstone designs, Momma D burned with rage. She was angry at Tina, the gunman, and the police. But the person she blamed most was herself. Had she reacted differently years ago—shown more compassion—maybe this wouldn't have happened.

Three years earlier, long before Terran's drug-related escapades had come to light, one of Momma D's social work colleagues had warned her about Tina's then-casual drug use. Oblivious to how childhood trauma might be driving her niece's erratic behavior, Ms. Dana had gone ballistic, openly berating Tina for defiling her mother's memory and threatening to cut her off if she didn't get her shit together. Instead of drawing her back into the fold, the exchange had had the opposite effect. Tina had retreated—crack was stronger than tough love—and abruptly severed all family ties. Upon learning that Tina and her daughter had been using together for months, Ms. Dana couldn't help but wonder: if she'd been more patient, more supportive with Tina, might her own child be alive today?

As Dana's mother and siblings vacillated between anger and sarcasm to ease the pain, the Lawton grandchildren expressed their grief in different but equally troubling ways. After a few months, Terran Sr. and Malia noticed that while Tyler's nighttime cries for Momma had subsided, he was speaking less and less. When TJ began wetting the bed, the newly formed parenting partnership sought counseling together. (To no one's surprise, after weeks of back and forth in family court, Terran had "agreed" to share custody of the boys with their relentless aunt.) Dana's nieces and nephews also were exhibiting concerning effects of the loss. Age-appropriate responses ranged from quiet brooding and oddly timed temper tantrums to light truancy, including Damon sneaking out one night to spray-paint his auntie's name on the side of a parked police cruiser.

No matter how uncomfortable the interactions, Tina endured and continued to show up—it was the least she could do. She was even present that first Easter Sunday after the incident, when, for the first time anyone could remember, Dana's brothers and sisters had to cook the meal: Momma D never got out of bed.

The most upsetting display of angst Tina witnessed was that of Terran Sr. Tina was on her way to the 27th Street bus stop—yeah, *that* bus stop—a few months after authorities had discovered Dana's body. As she crossed the busy intersection against traffic, Little Jackie, a baby-faced dealer with a wicked stutter, intercepted her before she could take a seat.

"Hey, T-T-Tina. Ya-ya need to get your boy," he spat. "Been here an hour, just sittin'. Ain't tryna cop nothin'. Brotha's 'round here gettin' nervous."

Tina had seen Terran weeks earlier at the barbershop with his boys and his new girlfriend, the "Rehab Ho," Dana had called her.

As she mumbled a stiff, "Hello," kneeling down to embrace the kids, Tina didn't hide her contempt for the woman who had "loved" away Terran's crack habit when his wife and children could not. Terran was less talkative than usual, but otherwise, he seemed fine. *What a difference a few days make.*

Terran's car was parked in the far corner of the gravel lot, within earshot of conversations on the bench, facing the graffiti-covered brick wall. As Tina approached, she could see the stream of thick black smoke floating up out of the open driver-side window.

"Terran," Tina called out so as not to startle him. "What'chu got there?"

As their eyes met, Tina gasped. Her cousin's husband looked terrible! He'd lost a scary amount of weight. His face was sunken, his hair was wild and dusted with soot, and his eyes were severely bloodshot. At first, Terran seemed not to recognize her, but soon something between a smirk and a smile flashed across his face.

"What's up?" he asked so softly she could barely make out the words. "I'm just resting for a minute. I had some stuff to take care of. Don't get excited. I'm not using. But I am a little drunk."

"It's cold as shit out here," Tina said with a chuckle to lighten the mood as she opened the passenger door. What she saw next nearly took her breath away.

On the passenger seat was a silver bowl, a wedding gift from Terran's now-deceased grandfather and the place from which the dense smoke emanated. Terran was setting fire to photos from his wedding album! The wind from the now-open door wasn't strong enough to extinguish the fire, but the sudden gust sent blue-gray ashes flying across the windshield. The pungent scent of burning photo paper made Tina gag, but Terran didn't seem to notice. Blinking, he wiped a tear from his cheek and placed another image on the fire.

"I burned us, Tina," he said. "By bringing that poison into our home, I burned it all down. How can I ever explain this to my boys?"

Tina grabbed an old towel from the back seat, smothered the fire, and placed the charred bowl outside on the gravel. Moving ever so slowly, she climbed into the car and closed the door. As she watched Terran scrape specs of soot from a scorched five-by-seven of his now-dead wife and their first-born son, something inside Tina broke. *What a waste of a beautiful black family.*

She stayed with Terran for another half-hour, staring at the brick wall, not speaking, finally allowing her pent up tears to flow. As her ever-present cravings for crack burned deep within, she wondered. For months, Dana had been searching for a way to get out of the life and save her boys. Well, she was out. Technically, her death had been ruled a homicide. *Maybe,* Tina thought with a shudder, *it was something else entirely?*

Tina had reason to wonder. One Sunday morning, about a month before Thanksgiving, MJ's overnight guests had been startled awake by the most unlikely of sounds: gospel music playing in the alley. While everyone else covered their heads, Dana and Tina crawled over passed-out bodies and peeked through the spaces between the room-darkening curtains. There, next to the burned-out Buick where the crackheads hid old clothes, Pastor Mac and about 10 church members had erected a pop-up sanctuary.

Dana and Tina were too embarrassed to go outside, but they had no problem listening. Music gave way to the preached Word, and the window-sill congregation grew as others in the house moved closer. Pretty much everyone there knew Dana Lawton considered herself a Christian. The girl called on the name of the Lord often, especially when she crashed. Still, they were shocked to hear her speak from memory as Pastor Mac quoted the key verse of the day: "Death is gain because death means more of Christ, and he's better than anything this life can give us" (Philippians 1:22–23).

Less than an hour later, after heartfelt intercessory prayer by a tall, heavily tattooed former prostitute, the alley was once again silent. Inside, reactions were mixed. Some disregarded the service entirely, mocking both pastor and prostitute for the holier-than-thou display.

"I *know* that ho," one man joked. "She's got a lot of nerve standing up in front like that."

Others either exchanged hearty "Hallelujahs" and "Amens" as they debated what they'd heard or nervously exited the scene without comment. For the most part, the believers in the group received the message as a metaphorical reference to the death of one's sinful nature. Dana, Tina recalled, didn't hear it that way.

"Death is gain," she'd repeated emphatically. "So, dying can be repentance. And once you repent, you can be redeemed to God."

"I don't know," Tina had cautioned. "So, you have to die to be saved? That don't sound right."

"Whatever," Dana had replied. "God said it. I believe it."

As Terran's car exited the parking lot and disappeared around the corner, Tina sat down hard on the bus stop bench. Transaction made, she closed her eyes and took a long drag on the pipe, desperate to blot out the faces of the loved ones now destined to endure this agony for years to come.

If what happened here really was some kind of fucked up spiritual detox, she thought, *and all these shattered lives are just unavoidable casualties of a redeemed soul, well...count me out.*

♥

Afterword

A T ITS CORE, *THE SIN-SICK SOUL* IS A COMPILATION of true-to-life anecdotes, imagination and innuendo, supplemented by research. This approach—part fact/part fiction—was, in my assessment, the only way to convey both the authenticity and complexity of such an easy-to-misdiagnose circumstance that impacts the lives of so many young people.

I believe it is safe to conclude that there are many instances of partners of addicts who experiment with the drug as an act of revenge. While specific situations differ, the anger and guilt these spurned lovers experience are likely universal. But, I contend, romantic partners aren't the only ones susceptible to self-destruction after someone they love dies from addiction. Parents blame each other, and long-term marriages fail. Siblings blame the "system," reject authority, and turn to crime. And the most innocent victims, children of deceased addicts, live in a constant state of emotional confusion, not knowing who to blame. It is this last group for whom I have the greatest concern and whose long-term prognosis is most difficult to predict.

Real-world outcomes often defy logic: a pre-teen who was old enough to experience first-hand the chaos of a parent's addiction reaches adulthood substance-free, while a toddler whose memories of Momma are little more than shadows descends into full-fledged addiction before his 13th birthday. For caregivers standing in the gap, it is terrifying to acknowledge that no one knows how to save these kids. But whether it's crack cocaine, opioids, or something new, for the sake of our children, we must never stop asking the tough questions, questions such as:

1. Are there historical lessons about how society has mishandled addiction that leaders today are ignoring at our peril?

Consider the hypothesis raised in 2015 by renowned writer Ta-Nehisi Coates: In the late 1980s, the crack cocaine epidemic had ravaged America, with thousands of overdoses and murders associated with the drug trade each year. If the United States had responded to this crisis by investing in drug addiction treatment, an infrastructure would already be in place to address such a crisis—an infrastructure that could have endured to this day. This critical architecture might have prevented one of the greatest challenges to the current opioid crisis—only about 10 percent of people with a drug use disorder—and an even lower percentage of children of addicts — receive specialized treatment. But unfortunately, since crack largely afflicted black communities, the response at the time was not public health-oriented. Instead, leaders focused almost entirely on criminalizing addiction by passing laws to incarcerate dealers and users in mass through exorbitant prison sentences dictated by mandatory minimums, an approach that many policymakers now consider a mistake. As a result, the United States has been playing catch-up as we rush to establish the treatment systems we need to tackle the current crisis.[4]

Point taken, Coates. Criminalizing addiction didn't work then, and it doesn't work now.

2. Do "tough love" treatment programs work?

The fictional Squash It program that saved the life of Dana's husband, Terran, was borne out of a distillation of information from staff interviews, promotional materials, and rare testimonials by a few recovering crack addicts of the day who, against the backdrop of criminalization and shame described previously, possessed the discipline and courage to seek various treatment methods. While what works appears to be highly personal, experts continue to debate the long-term effectiveness of anti-drug programs that promote the stern, sometimes even harsh, treatment of users to force personal responsibility.

Reference a November 1981 *People Magazine* article that chronicled an often-referenced case study supporting such practices:

Phyllis and David York had three daughters, all of whom had fallen into drug addiction. When one of the daughters was arrested a second time for a drug-related crime—this time for robbing a cocaine dealer—the Yorks had had enough. They refused to bail their daughter out of jail, and they would not visit her. After being locked up for six weeks, they acquitted the daughter; but the parents still would not allow her to return home until she agreed to seek help for her addiction. After four months in a halfway house, the contrite teen was on her way to recovery, while her parents continued to suffer. It is this ordeal that motivated the Yorks to found *TOUGH LOVE*, a support group to help parents navigate the myriad of conflicting emotions that accompany efforts to "do what you think is best" for a troubled child.

"We are not advising you to stop caring about your teenager," Tough Love founders David and Phyllis York wrote in their self-help manual for parents. "But we are suggesting you stop treating your young person like a poor, helpless child."[5]

On the flip side, other researchers contend that, for chronic addicts, isolation tactics such as those the Yorks' daughter was subjected to may do more harm than good. An excerpt from the 2018 psychcentral.com blog post by David M. Kolker offers a powerful justification for this antithetical point of view:

I recently met a family whose daughter is a client and whose son had recently died from a heroin overdose. The father told me, "we are here to get help for our daughter, she is a heroin addict." He recounted a story of "tough love" regarding his son who died of a heroin overdose four months prior, at age 23. Mr. Jones stated his son had been admitted to seven Florida drug rehab programs between the ages of 18-23, and the longest period of sobriety he could attain was 11 months clean.

"My son was plagued, he wanted to stop, he asked for help repeatedly and in the face of all the professionals, we continued to attempt to help," he stated. "Finally, we gave in and decided that 'tough love' was the answer. We would no longer accept our son's phone calls, refused to provide financial support, and let him hit rock bottom. The professionals told us this was the only way, and we listened. The result for us was that our son died of an overdose in a McDonald's bathroom, alone."

Mr. Jones stated, "I blame myself for giving up on my son and I won't make the same mistake twice. I have to live with the consequences, not the professionals who provide the same recommendations to every family."[6]

My take? When it's your son, your sister, your mother, only *you* can decide.

3. Suicide by murder: is it a myth or a legitimate woefully understudied phenomenon in addiction-related deaths?

WARNING: For the jump-to-the-end cheaters among you, I'm about to reveal the basic premise of this story: Dana Lawton is a "ghetto fabulous" young wife and mother living and loving life in the hood. Following a cocaine-fueled betrayal by her husband and high school sweetheart, she convinces herself the world would be a better place if she did not exist. But for a devout Christian, suicide is out of the question. Such an unthinkable act would not only damn her soul to hell; it would destroy her mother and torment her children for the rest of their lives. Now if someone *else* takes her life, that shields her babies from danger without expanding her already-massive repertoire of unforgiveable sins— problem solved!

On the surface, this warped logic reads like textbook depression, a common explanation as to why people kill themselves. But as I researched the high-profile suicides of celebrity chef Anthony Bourdain and fashion designer Kate Spade, I stumbled upon some thought-provoking insights by speaker/author Mark Goulston (*Just Listen,* Harper Collins, September 2009) that suggest a different explanation.

According to Goulston, its *des-pair*—that is, "being *unpaired* from the real world"—that consumes a suicidal person the moment before he or she jumps off the bridge or pulls the trigger. Admittedly, I found this point of view intriguing. But in this work of fiction, and in the real-life scenario from which the story was inspired, our heroine didn't kill *herself.* In fact, police records suggest she fought for her life until the very end. While, at some point in her journey, she undoubtedly felt despair, I contend it was impulsiveness that ultimately sealed Dana's fate. From the first inept inhale on her husband's crack pipe to that final, fatal snatch and dash, her true nemesis was her predilection to *act first, think later.* Dana didn't want to die. But she didn't want to live, either.

Had a viable third option presented itself, logic suggests she may have taken it.

Unfortunately, addiction is by no means logical.

AUTHOR'S NOTE

A Call to Action

LET'S FACE IT: the greatest medical and legal minds of our age likely will never agree on a universal right course of action when someone you love is addicted to drugs. But at the risk of oversimplification, I'll end this tale with a few rudimentary observations from family members of addicts, many of whom got clean and lived.

No one is immune to addiction. Seriously. The most vocal critic of illicit drug use is just one heartbreak away from popping a pill or firing up a pipe and changing his or her life forever. By the way, being broken by pain is *not* a character flaw.

Don't mind your own business. Older siblings, in particular, this one's for you. All your lives, you've kept every secret: his first bully on the playground, her first kiss, forbidden piercings, and tattoos.

This is not *that*. The transition from recreational to dependent drug user is often gradual. Pay attention, do your research, build a plan, and then say something. Choose your words carefully. Seek professional guidance. But whatever you do, don't wait to take action. Now is NOT the time to stop bossing them around.

And finally, forgive yourself. When it's all said and done, all you can do is all you can do.

♥

References

1. Puja Seth, Lawrence Scholl, Rose A. Rudd, Sarah Bacon. "Overdose Deaths Involving Opioids, Cocaine, and Psychostimulants—United States, 2015" (*CDC Morbidity and Mortality Weekly Report*, March 2018).
2. Jennifer A. Hoffmann; Caitlin A. Farrell, Michael C. Monuteaux, et al. "Association of Pediatrics Suicide with County-Level Poverty in the United States 2007–2016."
3. Gregory Jordan. *Safe At Home: The Willie Mays Aikens Story* (Triumph Books, May 1, 2012).
4. Ta-Nehisi Coates. "The Black Family in the Age of Mass Incarceration" (*The Atlantic*, October 2015).
5. Caleb Neuhaus, "David and Phyllis York Treat Problem Teen with a Dose of Tough Love" (People.com, November 1981).
6. David M. Kolker. "Does Tough Love Lead to Wellness?" (Psychcentral.com, July 2018).